Love at the Soda Fountain

ROSE ASH

ARCHWAY
PUBLISHING

Archway Publishing books may be ordered
through booksellers or by contacting:

Archway Publishing
1663 Liberty Drive
Bloomington, IN 47403
www.archwaypublishing.com
1 (888) 242-5904

ISBN: 978-1-4808-7470-1 (sc)
ISBN: 978-1-4808-7471-8 (hc)
ISBN: 978-1-4808-7472-5 (e)

Library of Congress Control Number: 2019902682

Print information available on the last page.

Archway Publishing rev. date: 03/27/2019

For Mom and Aunt Sally

Chapter 1

1964

Elizabeth clutched her heart as she hung up the phone and quickly sat down at the kitchen table. She breathed deeply, trying to calm down. Dylan walked in, carrying his homework. He grabbed a Pepsi out of the fridge and then glanced over at his mom. "Mom, what's wrong? Are you okay?"

"Your sister's going to put me in the grave. I just can't believe it. What did I do wrong?" Elizabeth took a sip of water. She didn't feel well. Dylan rubbed her back.

"Who's causing the problem this time, Sarah or Brenda?" He sat down at the table.

"Sarah. She's on her way to Elkton, to marry Robert at the Wedding Chapel."

"Why on earth is she doing that? Driving all the way from Connecticut to Maryland to get married?"

"It's probably because I wouldn't let her wear her engagement ring. I kept telling her she was too young to get married. She's making the biggest mistake of her life. She's only twenty."

"Dad's going to go nuts when he finds out. I got to go tell Teddy."

"I'm going to lie down awhile. What a scandal this is."

"You sure you're going to be okay?" Dylan asked.

"Yes, yes. Go tell Teddy. The whole town will know soon anyway," Elizabeth said. She stood up and walked down to her bedroom. She heard Dylan open the back door and race down the stairs to the Smiths' place. Elizabeth and her family rented from Dr. Smith and his family who lived below them.

What on earth had gotten into Sarah? Elizabeth thought as she lay down on her bed. She was too young to get married. Elizabeth herself had waited until her thirties. It wasn't that Elizabeth didn't like Robert. She liked him a lot. Sarah had met him at a dance at the Episcopal Church right down the road, when they had both been fifteen. They loved dancing together and had even won dance competitions at the Laurelville Fair. But Elizabeth had always wondered about Robert's lifestyle. He sometimes hung out with unusual men.

Elizabeth lay there, her thoughts racing. She heard the front door open and close. It was Eugene, coming home from work. She knew he wasn't going to take this news well.

"Elizabeth, Elizabeth, where are you?"

"In the bedroom."

"What are you doing in the bedroom? You feeling okay? You look pale." He sat down on the bed next to her.

"I'm not feeling very well," Elizabeth said. "Sarah just called. She's on her way to Maryland."

"Why? I thought she was working at the pharmacy today."

"I thought she was working too. She's eloping with Robert. That's why she's on her way to Maryland."

"Why on earth is she doing that? Is she pregnant?"

"Oh no, I never thought of that. I pray that that isn't the case, pregnant at her age? I can't believe this. What a scandal this will be if that's true. Eloping is embarrassing enough." Elizabeth turned white and clutched her heart again.

Chapter 2

Sarah hung up the pay phone outside of the restaurant. She and Robert had stopped in New Jersey to eat. Her mom hadn't seemed to take the news too badly. She walked back into the Howard Johnson's and smiled at Robert as she sat down in the booth across from him. "How'd they take the news?" Robert asked.

"Mom answered. She didn't say much. She didn't even yell. She was actually super quiet."

"That's probably just the calm before the storm. Plus, it's your mom's own fault. She wouldn't even let you wear the engagement ring I got you. She kept saying you were too young to be engaged. Plenty of girls get engaged and then married at twenty." Robert grabbed Sarah's left hand and touched the top of the diamond. The ring glistened in the sunlight as he moved it back and forth. "I like your mom, but she sure was stubborn about us getting married."

Sarah sipped on her chocolate shake. She felt nervous. She'd thought eloping would make her feel good, but it confused her. She was an adult. She could do what she wanted. She tried not to let it bother her that her family wasn't going to see her get married. She loved Robert. He was the best friend she'd ever had next to her older sister Brenda. She wished she could talk to Brenda. Was she making a mistake?

"Hey, don't look sad. Everything will be fine. She'll come around." Robert stroked Sarah's hand. The waitress brought their food over. Sarah was famished. She felt better after eating.

"We're about halfway there. We just need to fill up with gas and then we can head out. We've been lucky that we haven't hit much traffic." Robert took a bite of his burger.

"I'm excited, Robert. The Wedding Chapel is famous. And it's great that your mom is going to get the keys to our apartment while we're gone."

"Yes, and they'll move in everything. Can you believe my parents and grandparents bought all the furniture for our place?"

"It is nice of them."

"How you going to feel about living above a package store?"

"It doesn't bother me at all. At least it isn't a bar. Plus, we've got a view of the river."

"You've always loved water. Don't know what it's about you and water," Robert said.

I do love water Sarah thought. She was looking forward to living with Robert but also was a little nervous. She was thrilled about being able to be right next to the river. Plus, it would only be about a ten-minute drive to the pharmacy.

"Can I get you guys anything else?" the waitress asked.

"Nope, we'll take the check," Robert said.

"I won't take your money. This one's on me. I heard you're getting married tomorrow. Congratulations!"

"Thanks so much," Sarah said. She gave the woman a big smile.

"Young love. Ain't nothing like it. I've been married almost twenty years myself. Are your parents meeting you down there?"

"Nope, they can't make it," Sarah said.

"Why?"

"Too busy. And my mom thinks I'm too young."

"Don't worry, kid. She'll come around. You guys take care."

Chapter 3

Dylan hoped Teddy was back from his class. Sarah eloping with Robert was quite the news. Mrs. Smith opened the door. "Well, Dylan. Come on in. What's going on?"

"You won't believe it. Sarah's eloping with Robert. I have to tell Teddy."

"Eloping? Are you serious? Sarah's such a good girl."

"I'm serious. She just called and said she's on her way to Elkton. Is Teddy here?"

"Nope, he headed up to the pharmacy just a few minutes ago. He said he was in the mood for a chocolate shake. You could probably catch him."

"I'll do that. Thanks Mrs. Smith."

On Main Street, he saw Teddy way up ahead. "Teddy, Teddy, wait!"

Teddy stopped and turned. Dylan came running up to him. "You'll never guess what."

"What?"

"Sarah's eloping with Robert."

"You have got to be kidding." Teddy broke into a laugh. "Is your mom freaked out or what?"

"She's a mess. I feel bad for her."

"Hey, I'm on my way to the pharmacy; let's see if they knew about it."

Dylan loved visiting the pharmacy. The owners, Laura and Henry, were like family. Next door was a bakery from where everyone in town got their birthday cakes. The pharmacy's parking lot always smelled like chocolate chip cookies and bread.

Dylan waved at Heather, Sarah's best friend, who worked at the soda fountain when she wasn't taking classes at Milltown Community College. Dylan thought Heather was one of the prettiest and smartest girls in town. She wasn't like other girls. She was serious and knew she wanted to be a pharmacist.

"Hi guys! What can I get you?" Heather asked.

"I'll take a chocolate milkshake," Teddy said.

"I'll have a coffee shake." Dylan beckoned to her to come closer. She leaned into Dylan. His heart raced.

"Do you know where Sarah is?"

"No, I don't and why on earth are you whispering?" Heather went over to scoop out ice cream for their shakes.

"Don't you think it's odd she's not working?" Dylan asked.

"No. She just asked me to cover today and tomorrow for her. She said she had some stuff she had to do." Sarah poured milk into the cups before mixing up their shakes. Henry and Laura came over from the counter.

"What are you guys up to?" Laura asked.

"We've got some news about Sarah." Dylan took his shake from Heather.

"What's wrong with Sarah? Is she okay?" Henry looked concerned.

"She's on her way to Elkton, with Robert. They're eloping."

"What? I had no idea." Laura looked startled. "Why wouldn't she tell us? Robert's in here all the time visiting when she's working. We love Robert. They didn't need to elope."

"My mother was quite upset, and she has a bad heart." Dylan took a sip of his shake. "I wonder if Sarah did it because my mom wouldn't let her wear the ring Robert got her. My mom thinks she's too young to get married."

"I wonder if Robert's parents know," Henry said.

Chapter 4

Robert glanced over at Sarah as he drove. She was asleep. She was the love of his life. He couldn't believe they were doing this. He was thrilled. He couldn't wait to live with Sarah and not have to live with his parents anymore. He didn't mind living with his dad, but his mom's alcoholism was getting to him. She had been an alcoholic for as long as he could remember. She was often drunk and when she was, she verbally abused anyone around her and it was often Robert. He'd never understood her behavior, because he always tried to be there to help her. His mom's behavior had impacted his whole life. He couldn't take friends to his house if she was drunk. Sarah had provided Robert with the love and support he needed. He longed for his own place with Sarah, so he could have peace and tranquility.

Robert pulled into the YWCA parking lot. Sarah woke when he stopped the car. She stretched. "Are we here?"

"We sure are, sleepy head. I loved watching you sleep."

"I had a nice nap. I dreamed of us having lots of babies," Sarah said. "I can't wait to have children."

"You'll make a great mom. You've always loved children."

"I wish my mom thought that. You know she wanted me to become a pharmacist and then get married and have babies. That's not me. Just because she was a rarity for her time as a working woman, it doesn't mean I need to follow the same path. I want babies."

"I know. Pharmacy school would take a lot of time. Look how hard Heather's working just to get ready to go."

There was an older woman sitting at a desk at the entrance of the YWCA. "Can I help you?

"Yes, I'm Sarah Jones and I have a room reservation." Sarah looked around the lobby which was sparsely decorated.

The woman looked down at her sheet. "Yes, I see you here on the list. It's ten dollars for the night and I just need you to sign here."

Sarah signed on the line the woman pointed to. Robert smiled at the woman as he gave her the ten dollars. Even though Sarah acted tough, Robert could tell Sarah was nervous. She kept wringing her hands. Robert loved the contradictions Sarah often presented. She always tried acting tough, but Robert knew she was a marshmallow underneath.

"You want to put anything back on your assigned bed? My name is Jessica in case you need anything."

"I'll bring my stuff in when I come back."

"Okay. Sounds like a plan. See you when you come back."

"Thanks." Sarah grabbed Robert's hand as they headed out to the car.

"It's a bummer we have to stay separately tonight," Robert said. He longed to spend the night with Sarah.

"It's just one more night." Sarah squeezed his hand. Robert drove over to the YMCA where he checked into his room. They then headed to the marriage license office where they had their blood drawn and filled out all the needed forms.

"You guys are all set. You can come back tomorrow at noon and get your license," the clerk said to them.

"Thanks. Let's go check out the chapel." Robert grabbed Sarah's hand.

"What chapel you getting married at?" the clerk asked.

"The Wedding Chapel. Is it close by?"

"Oh, that place is so cute. Yes, it's right down the road about one mile on the left."

"Thanks again." Sarah followed Robert out the door. Robert drove down to the Wedding Chapel.

Two couples were waiting in the reception area of the chapel with their families. Robert was surprised at how crowded it was, but this was where a lot of people eloped to because of Maryland's marriage laws. The Wedding Chapel was famous.

A woman came walking into the reception area from the back. "Hi there, can I help you? I'm Olive."

"Hi, I'm Robert and this is Sarah, we spoke with you on the phone earlier." Olive looked at her appointment book.

"Oh yes, from Connecticut. I have you down for tomorrow at one o'clock."

"That's right. Do we need to do anything before tomorrow?"

"Just bring your marriage license and flowers if you like. We can take the photos for you. Do have any family coming?"

"No, no we don't," Sarah replied. Robert saw the disappointment in Sarah's face. He knew she wished her family was there, especially her sister Brenda.

Chapter 5

Brenda got out of her bright red Chevy Impala convertible that she loved driving with the top down. She wondered what was for dinner. She was tired and hungry. She'd had a late night at the cinema with her best friend Eva Marie and had been tired at work all day.

No one was around in the family room. Her dad was usually sitting there watching the evening news. Brenda popped her head around the corner and looked around the kitchen. To Brenda's surprise there was no sign of food anywhere and nothing was cooking on the stove. Where was everyone? She spotted a note on the fridge. *Your mom isn't feeling good. Took her to Milltown Hospital Emergency Room. Dylan took off somewhere with Teddy. When he comes back cook some hot dogs for dinner. I think your mom will be fine so just stay there. Love, Dad.*

What the heck is going on? And where was Sarah? She was usually home by now. Maybe she's working. Brenda picked up the phone and dialed the pharmacy.

"Hi Laura. This is Brenda. Is my sister up there working tonight?"

"No, she's not. Dylan's here though. Want to talk to him?"

"Sure." Brenda twirled the phone cord while she waited for Dylan to come to the phone.

"Hey, sis."

"What are you doing up there? What's going on? Dad left

a note saying he took Mom to the emergency room. Do you know what's wrong?"

"Oh no. She told me she was fine. She went to lie down. The news really shook her up."

"What news?"

"Did the note say anything else?"

"No."

"Okay, I'll be right there." Dylan hung up before Brenda could ask him any more questions. She hoped their mom was okay. Maybe she would go to the hospital and take Dylan with her. She poured some Pepsi into a glass and sat down at the table.

After about ten minutes, Dylan rushed in with Teddy.

"Dylan, Teddy, what on earth's going on?"

"Wait until you hear this. Sarah and Robert are eloping." Dylan watched his sister's face closely. She looked shocked.

"What? She wouldn't elope without telling me. Are you pulling my leg?"

"No, he isn't. They didn't even know about it at the pharmacy," Teddy said.

"I can't believe she's done this to me. She's my sister. Why didn't she tell me?"

"What's going on with Mom? She said she was going to lie down when I left."

"Why did you leave her?"

"She said she was fine," Dylan replied.

"She always says she's fine. Did Sarah even consider how this would impact Mom? Sometimes she's so selfish." Brenda pulled out the phone book.

"I'm calling the hospital to see if I can find out how she's doing. Go tell Teddy's mom what's going on. Give me some space."

Brenda knew Dylan and Teddy got a little scared of her when she was annoyed. They rushed out the back door.

Brenda was glad they were gone. She was having a difficult time processing everything. She found the main number for the hospital and dialed it. "Milltown Hospital, can I help you?"

"Hi. Yes. My name is Brenda Jones and my dad Eugene Jones brought my mother Elizabeth Jones to the emergency room recently. Can you possibly connect me so I can see how she's doing?"

"I can. Hold on please." Brenda heard the phone click and ring at another line.

"Emergency room. Can I help you?"

"Yes, my name is Brenda Jones. My dad Eugene Jones is there with my mom. Is there any way I can speak to him?"

"Okay. Let me put you on hold and see if I can find him." Brenda sat down and waited. Suddenly she heard her dad's voice on the other end of the phone. "Dad, is that you?"

"Brenda. Don't worry. They say your mom's going to be fine. They think that stress caused her blood pressure to skyrocket but it's come down. They gave her a minor tranquilizer. We'll be heading home in a few minutes."

Chapter 6

Sarah's alarm clock woke her from a deep sleep. She knocked if off the nightstand. "Oops," she said, as she bent down and picked up the clock and shut it off. She'd slept well. She was excited but also confused. Eloping wasn't as fun as she'd thought it would be. She wished she could talk to Brenda. She was sad that her family wasn't there with her to celebrate. Robert had told her eloping was the only way they could be together. They were meeting for breakfast and then she would come back to get dressed for her wedding. She got ready and Robert picked her up.

"I'm starved. There's a breakfast place down the road." Robert grabbed Sarah's hand.

"How did you sleep?" Sarah asked.

"Really well. How about you?"

"I couldn't fall asleep at first but then I totally passed out and didn't wake until the alarm clock went off."

Robert pulled into a pancake place and opened his car door. "Come on, beautiful, let's eat and then go get the flowers."

The pancake place was quite crowded. "How long of a wait?" Robert asked the hostess.

"Is it just the two of you?"

"Yes." Robert smiled at Sarah.

"It'll be just a couple minutes. I need to clean off a small booth that I have in the back." Sarah spotted a man sitting by himself at a booth facing towards the door. She tapped Robert on the arm. "Hey that looks like Gary from church over there in the booth, doesn't it?" Robert looked over; his body tensed. He started sweating.

"Isn't that him?" Sarah asked.

"I don't think so."

"I swear it's him. Do you think he's following us?"

"Don't be ridiculous."

The hostess returned and took them to a booth way back in the restaurant. "Your waitress will be right with you."

"I swear, Robert, that looked just like Gary. Did my parents send him here to spy on us?"

"No way. It wasn't Gary. Just forget about it and figure out what you want." Robert looked at his menu. Sarah wondered why his mood had changed. What was going on?

Chapter 7

"I have to use the bathroom. I'll be right back," Robert said. He walked up toward the front of the restaurant, making sure Sarah couldn't see him. He walked over to Gary's table.

"Surprise. Bet you didn't expect to see me here," Gary said.

"Meet me in the men's room in a couple minutes."

"Aren't you demanding?" Gary said. Robert walked into the men's restroom. No one else was in there. He paced back and forth until Gary showed up.

"Wanted to be alone with me?" Gary asked.

"What on earth are you doing in Maryland? Are you crazy? Sarah's going to see you."

"I don't care if Sarah sees me. She won't care if I'm here. She knows nothing about us."

"As I told you before, Gary, I'm marrying Sarah and nothing or no one is going to stop me."

"You don't really want to marry her. You're just caving to societal pressures."

"I am not. I love Sarah. She gives me stability."

"She may do that, but there's more than that to life." Gary went to the sink and washed his hands.

"What do you want from me, Gary?" Robert asked.

"I don't want you to marry Sarah. You're making a huge

mistake. It's not fair to her if you marry her. You have a double life."

"Shut up, Gary. I don't have a double life. I'm marrying Sarah and we're going to have children."

"Oh, the perfect American dream. You won't be happy. She can't protect you from your demons."

Robert pushed Gary against the wall. "Leave me alone, Gary. Leave me alone. Get out of Elkton. Now!"

"Don't you bully me," Gary said. Robert loosened his grip. "I will leave, but you know you won't be rid of me. You sure piss me off. You're making a huge mistake."

Chapter 8

$\mathcal{B}$renda and Dylan jumped up from the couch when their mom and dad walked through the door. Elizabeth looked exhausted. Brenda hugged her mom. "Are you okay? What happened?"

"I'm fine, Brenda. I think the news of Sarah eloping just threw me for a loop," Elizabeth replied.

"Mom, here. sit down." Dylan pulled out a chair for her.

"Got any hot dogs left?" Eugene asked.

"Yes, Dad, let me get you and Mom some food. I just can't believe Sarah didn't tell me any of this. I'm so angry with her. I would have liked to have been at her wedding. What's her problem?"

"She's too young to be doing this. But what's done is done. We found out that Robert's parents knew all about it. Your dad called them for me. I guess they have an apartment all ready when they return, overlooking the river."

"What? You mean she isn't even coming back to stay at all?" Brenda said. "I can't believe Sarah did this to me. We share everything with one another. When is she coming back?"

"We aren't quite sure. Robert's parents said that after Maryland they're going on a honeymoon to New York City," Elizabeth replied.

"Do you think she's pregnant or something?' Brenda asked.

"Brenda, my word." Elizabeth sipped her water.

"It's possible. Think about it. Otherwise she'd want us there with her."

"You're just mad because now you're the old maid, sis." Dylan slapped Brenda playfully on the back.

"Dylan, don't be ugly." Elizabeth stood up. She put her arm around her daughter. "Brenda, honey, come on in the living room with me. Let's watch a movie or something and get our minds off this. It's been a stressful day."

"Alright, Mama."

Chapter 9

Sarah showered and put on her white dress. It was knee-length, sleeveless and had gorgeous lace trim. Her brunette hair was a beautiful contrast to the dress. She put on her white heels and the pearl necklace and earrings that Robert had gotten her as an engagement present. Next, she did her makeup, applying bright red lipstick. She packed her bag and headed out to the lobby area. She gasped when she spotted Robert in his black suit. He looked so handsome.

"Wow. Do you look fantastic." Robert gave her a kiss on the cheek and grabbed her bag.

"You do too. This is so exciting," Sarah went up to the desk and handed the clerk her key.

"Good luck today, you two. I hope you have a wonderful life together," the woman said.

"Can I help you guys?" the clerk said to Robert and Sarah as they walked into the flower shop. The shop smelled wonderful. Sarah loved the colors of the beautiful arrangements.

"We're getting married at the Wedding Chapel and we'd like to get a bouquet for Sarah and a boutonniere for me," said Robert.

After getting the flowers, Robert and Sarah drove over to the Wedding Chapel. The parking lot was much emptier than it had been the day before. Robert pulled in and parked.

"I'm so excited." He grabbed Sarah's hand and gazed into her eyes. "I love you so much."

"And I you." Sarah leaned in and gave Robert a passionate kiss. They got out of the car and Sarah took the boutonniere out of the back seat. She pinned it on Robert. He laughed and then took the boxes with the rings in them out of the glove compartment. He handed Sarah one of the ring boxes as they walked toward the chapel.

"Great to see you both again. I love your flowers, Sarah," said Olive. "We're all ready for you."

Two men stood and approached them. "Hi, I'm Ken. I'll be marrying you. I'm the justice of the peace. I'm happy for you both."

"And I'm Richard. I'm one of your witnesses. Heard you came all the way down from Connecticut. I love Connecticut, especially Sunflower Orchards." Richard shook Robert's hand.

"That's right near where we live."

"You can't get an apple pie that good anywhere else."

"That is so true." Sarah shook Richard's hand.

"You look very beautiful," Richard said.

"Thank you." Sarah blushed.

"Come on back," Olive said.

"Alright, let's begin," Ken said. "Welcome on this joyful day. Sarah and Robert, we are all glad that you came to the Wedding Chapel to be married. Robert, please take Sarah's ring and turn towards Sarah. Sarah, you turn towards Robert. Sarah, do you take Robert to have and to hold, from this day forward, for better, for worse, for richer, for poorer, in sickness and health, until death do you part?"

"I do." Sarah squeezed Robert's hand as she spoke. Robert put the ring on Sarah's finger. Olive took a photo.

"Sarah, please take Robert's ring. Now Robert, do you take Sarah to have and to hold, from this day forward, for better, for worse, for richer, for poorer, in sickness and health, until death do you part?"

"I do." Robert was overwhelmed with emotion, tears forming in his eyes as Sarah slipped the ring on his finger. Olive snapped another photo.

"Now, by the power vested in me, I pronounce you man and wife. You may kiss the bride," Robert moved in and gave Sarah a long, hard kiss. Tears of happiness streamed down his face. He heard the song by the Tymes, *So Much in Love*, playing in the background. Ken and Richard congratulated the couple. Olive took more photos. Suddenly, bells sounded as the front door opened and another couple walked in. Robert looked at Sarah.

"Wow, that was a quicker wedding than I thought it would be," Sarah said as she glanced hesitantly at the couple standing near the front door of the chapel. Robert could tell she was disappointed. He also knew that she really missed her family, even if she wouldn't admit it. He put his arm around her. She nestled her head in his shoulder.

"The length of time of a marriage ceremony isn't what's important. It's your commitment to one another," said Olive. "Let me go print these photos for you and put them in a little album. We'll get your bill settled and then you can be off. Congratulations you two!" She winked at Sarah, then turned to the couple who had just walked through the front door. "I'll be right with you."

Chapter 10

Brenda loved hanging out with Eva Marie on weekends when she worked at her friend's parents' store. Brenda would help her stock shelves and wait on customers. It was much more fun than her job as a secretary at the construction firm. She was saving the money she made to travel the world.

They were stocking shelves in the back when the bell jingled and the front door opened. Brenda turned and saw a tall man wearing an air force uniform. Brenda thought he was quite handsome. She nudged Eva Marie.

"Harry, what are on earth are you doing here?" Eva Marie ran towards the front of the store and gave the man a big hug. Brenda followed.

"Well, cousin, I came by to see how all of you were doing. Where's your mom and dad?" Harry asked as he smiled at Brenda. Brenda blushed and smiled back.

"This is my buddy, Brenda. My mom and dad are up at the high school volunteering at some sporting event. Brenda, this is my cousin Harry who's stationed in England."

Brenda put out her hand and Harry shook it. His hand felt warm. He smelled like Old Spice cologne. "I live up the road. I think we met when we were younger. I was probably covered in pimples and running around with my sister Sarah and my brother Dylan."

"Yes, I remember. I remember ice skating down at the pond. Nice to see you again. You're a lot taller."

"So are you," Brenda replied. They both laughed.

"Harry, why didn't you give us a heads up you were coming back?" Eva Marie asked.

"Well, I wasn't quite sure when I was getting leave. I just flew back last night and I slept later than usual because I'm still not used to the time change. It's tough going back and forth."

"Well, I'll let you guys catch up. See you around, Eva Marie," Brenda said.

"No, no. Why don't you stay a while, Brenda? I'd love to take you both out later to the pizza place if you want. And Eva Marie, if you're still dating Walter, bring him too." Harry lightly grabbed Brenda's arm. She felt a jolt of electricity. Eva Marie saw Brenda's reaction, gave her a funny look and winked.

"Yes, I'm still dating Walter. What do you think, Brenda?"

"Well, I need to get home and help my mom can some tomatoes, but I can meet you both at the pizza place. What time?"

"You name it, Eva Marie," Harry said.

"Let's say six o'clock."

"See you then." Brenda headed out the door with a big smile on her face. *This is going to be fun,* she thought.

Chapter 11

Robert and Sarah drove to New York City. They listened to a classical music station all the way. Robert had always loved classical music. Sarah didn't mind even though she preferred the popular hits. Robert had played piano and violin when he was younger. He was still pretty good at piano, but he hadn't practiced the violin in a long time. She loved it when he played the piano.

Sarah looked through the photos that Olive had taken. She'd put them in a cute little photo book that said, *Our Wedding* on the front in dark blue along with *Robert and Sarah, June 20, 1964*. Blue was Sarah's favorite color. She wondered if Robert knew that.

"Hey, Robert, what do think of the picture album Olive made?"

"I love it. The pictures came out great and you look terrific." Sarah sighed quietly. She wished her family, and especially Brenda, had been at the wedding. She knew Brenda was going to be upset. Sarah wished she could talk to her. Even though Brenda was her sister, she was one of her best friends too.

"We're almost there." Robert put his blinker on to get off at the next exit.

"I can't wait to see the hotel and the roof garden. Right on Times Square. Wow." Sarah pulled the visor down to check her make-up in the mirror. She took out her red lipstick and touched up her lips. Red looked terrific against her dark hair, dark eyes, and tan complexion. Robert stopped at the light.

"Gosh, this is going to be so romantic. I can't wait. You know I love New York City. Hey look. Wow. We're getting down into the heart of the city," Sarah said, pointing at the tall buildings. They were coming up to Times Square. There were people everywhere. Cars were honking. There were huge advertisements towering over the streets and overwhelming bright lights. Sarah loved the hustle and bustle of New York. Her family visited every year, to see the Rockettes. It was always a big treat. Robert pulled up in front of the hotel, under the canopy. A handsome valet in a black uniform came up to the car.

"Need help with your bags?" he asked Robert.

"Yes, please," Robert said as he got out of the car. He opened the trunk.

"Go ahead and check in and I'll meet you in there." The valet pulled his cart up to the back of the car.

"Oh Robert, this is so beautiful." Sarah kissed him. She grabbed his arm as they walked into the hotel. They walked up to the desk.

"Can I help you?"

"Yes, Mr. and Mrs. Robert Decker, checking in," Robert said.

Sarah smiled with delight. She couldn't believe she was Mrs. Robert Decker.

"Oh yes, we have you in the honeymoon suite, congratulations! You'll be on our top floor, facing Times Square. Just need you to sign here. You bill has been prepaid. You'll just need to cover any incidentals." Robert signed the check-in slip. The bellman walked up with the bags on the cart.

"Hope you enjoy your stay. Al will take you to your room and help you get settled. Here you go, Al, they're in room 1104."

"Thanks so much." Sarah smiled and turned and followed Al. He walked them toward the elevators. Sarah couldn't believe how big the hotel was; it had several hundred rooms. She was starting to get a little nervous because she'd never had sex with Robert before. She hoped it would be okay. Since she'd been home-schooled, she hadn't interacted much with boys, except when Dylan's friends came over or at church. Meeting Robert at church had been a blessing because he was so easy to talk to. They became best friends soon after meeting. They'd kissed every now and then but Robert had never pressured her for more.

"Wow," Sarah said when she saw the room. "This is huge. Robert, look at the roses and chocolates and the bottle of champagne."

Robert and the bellman smiled. There was a large bed in the room covered with a lace white bedspread. The furniture was dark so the bedspread stood out. There was a large desk and a loveseat facing a television on the dresser. Al set the bags on luggage holders. Robert gave him a tip.

"Thanks, hope you have a wonderful honeymoon."

"Oh Robert, this is like a dream." Sarah hugged and kissed him. He kissed her back hard.

"I'm so happy, Sarah." Robert ran his fingers through her hair.

"Me too." Sarah kissed him passionately then pulled away and threw open the curtain. "Oh my God, Robert, check out that view."

"Holy moly, it's Times Square."

"Look at all those lights."

"Good thing they got thick curtains," Robert said, "Hey, want to go walk around and then come back and have champagne and chocolate and have some fun?"

"Sure. Let me just freshen up and then we can head out."

Sarah unzipped her suitcase, got her toiletry bag, and walked into the bathroom. "Oh my God, it has marble floors."

Robert walked in to check out the bathroom. "This is the nicest bathroom I've ever seen. Check out the huge tub, we can have fun in that later."

Sarah gulped, she didn't look at Robert. She started sweating. She hoped the sex would be okay and not hurt too much. She had a new nightgown for the occasion. "You got a one-track mind; now get out of here so I can freshen up."

Chapter 12

*B*renda took the last jar of tomatoes out of the water with tongs. Elizabeth was almost done with the dishes. Brenda wiped sweat off her forehead. "Alright, Mom, that's the last one. Whew, I'm hot. I got to go take a shower."

"Where are you heading to?"

"Off to the pizza place to meet Eva Marie. Her cousin Harry's in town. He's home from England on leave."

"Oh good. The Rigonis are such a nice family. I know they worry about Harry. I'm glad he's home for a while. You go ahead and get ready. I'll finish up here."

Brenda took a long shower. It felt so good after canning tomatoes. She scrubbed her hands with lots of soap. She didn't want to smell like tomatoes. She still had her hair up in a towel when she walked over and opened her closet door. They were just going out for pizza so she had to make sure not to overdress. She pulled out her jeans and a nice white top. She took the towel off her head. She always wished her hair had been straight. You couldn't do much with curly hair, except let it dry naturally.

Dylan popped his head in her room. "Where you heading to, sis?"

"I'm meeting Eva Marie and some friends up at the pizza place."

"Can you drop me off at Rick's house on your way?"

"Yes, just be ready to go in about ten minutes."

"Thanks, sis, you're the best." Brenda put on a silver necklace and a silver ring her mother had given her. She worked more on her hair, trying to get the curls to fall into place. As she got ready, she thought more about Harry. She wondered if she found him so interesting because he was living in England. One of Brenda's goals in life was to travel the world. She put as much money as she could each week into a savings account. She couldn't wait to learn more about England from Harry that evening.

"Alright Dylan, come on, I'm ready," Brenda shouted as she walked down the hall.

"Great, let's go."

"See you, Mom," Brenda said.

"Dylan, where are you going?" Elizabeth asked from the kitchen.

"Over to Rick's to work on homework." Dylan kissed his mom on the head.

"How are you going to get back?"

"Rick's going to bring me home. We're going to hit the Dairy Serve on the way back."

"Do you think Mom's alright?" Dylan asked in the car. "With everything going on with Sarah?"

"She seemed okay when we were working on the tomatoes. I know her feelings are hurt. Heck, my feelings are hurt." Brenda stopped at a red light.

"Your feelings are hurt? Why?" Dylan asked.

"Because wouldn't you have wanted to be there? To be a part of it?" Brenda looked over at Dylan.

"Never thought of it that way. I'm just happy for her." Dylan switched the station on the radio.

"Well, I am happy for her," Brenda said as they pulled up at Rick's. "But I just wish I could have been there."

"Well, when she gets back, Henry and Laura at the pharmacy want to throw her a shower, so why don't we help?"

"That would be fun! I guess I shouldn't be mad. We could make it a surprise. Have fun. Tell Rick I said hi." Brenda changed the radio to a rock station. *I Can't Get No Satisfaction* came on and Brenda moved her body to the beat. She wondered where Sarah was right now. She wished she could talk to her. As she pulled into the parking lot, she saw that Eva Marie's car was already there. She checked her make-up in the mirror and then walked into the pizza place, waving at Eva Marie.

"Hi guys," Brenda said as she sat down.

"How was canning tomatoes?" Harry asked.

"Not bad. I just hope I don't smell like a tomato."

"Well, I think you smell great," Harry said. Brenda blushed.

"Hey, you didn't tell me Sarah eloped." Eva Marie took a sip of her Coke. Walter choked on his drink.

"What? Sarah eloped with Robert?" Walter asked.

"Yes. She called us on her way to Elkton." Brenda waved to get the waitress' attention. She was thirsty.

"Why didn't she have a regular wedding?" Eva Marie asked.

"Well, my mom wouldn't even let her wear her engagement ring. She said she was too young. I'll take a Coke," Brenda said to the waitress.

"You guys ready to order your pizza?"

"Brenda, we were going to order one onion and pepper pizza and one pepperoni. Is that okay with you?" Eva Marie asked.

"Fine with me." Brenda smiled at Harry. She thought he looked handsome. She wrung her hands under the table. She was a little nervous.

"Brenda, tell me about your job," Harry said.

"Well, it's not much. I work as a secretary at a construction company and then I'm taking part-time classes in business and photography."

"What do you like to photograph?" Harry smoothed back his hair. Brenda wondered if he was nervous too.

"Natural scenes. I especially love to photograph the ocean and lighthouses," Brenda said as the waitress put her Coke down.

"Well, I love the beach. Maybe some time we can go down to Hammonasset together and you can take some photos."

"I'd enjoy that." Brenda's heart raced. She took a sip of Coke. The waitress brought the pizzas over and they started eating.

"Wow, I miss American-made pizza. The pizza in England just isn't as good." Harry took another bite.

Walter turned towards Harry. "I don't know how you can stand living in England. I think it would be good at first but then a drag."

"I do get homesick, but trust me, they keep us super busy." Harry grabbed another piece of pizza.

"I'd love to see England. I've never traveled abroad. I'm saving to travel. I'd love to see Buckingham Palace and the changing of the guard," Brenda said.

"Well, maybe sometime you can come over there and see me." Harry winked and Brenda blushed again.

"I'd like that," she said.

Chapter 13

Robert held Sarah's hand as they left the diner. They walked around Times Square. The vibrant lights made the place feel exciting. Robert loved New York City. Sometimes he wished he could afford to live there. It was very liberal. He was married now. Sarah was his life. He'd made a choice.

"Wow, check out the skating rink," Sarah said.

"Want to go skating?" Robert asked.

"Yes, can we?"

"Of course, my love," Robert said. One of the things he loved most about Sarah was her enthusiasm for life. They rented skates and got onto the ice. Sarah was an excellent skater. She broke free from Robert's hand and started to twirl. He laughed as he watched her. She came up and grabbed his hand. He was so glad that they were married.

Next they went to the roof top bar on the top of their hotel. Sarah picked a table on the side that overlooked Times Square. The view was amazing. They both ordered gin and tonics. Sarah didn't usually drink much. Robert knew she was nervous about sex; it wasn't something they'd talked about. You couldn't talk much about sex. A band was playing dance music in the background. Couples were dancing.

"Robert, I love you so much," Sarah said.

"And I you. Skating was so much fun. You're an adventurer."

"I love New York City. This is such a treat. This place is gorgeous."

Robert noticed a group of young men sitting at the bar. They were laughing and having a good time. They were all neatly dressed. It looked as though they had just come from a show. Lots of couples were coming in to have drinks together.

"I love the way they dress here. Such different styles," Sarah said.

"I know. If we dressed like this back home, they would think we were crazy. We're two country bumpkins," Robert said.

"We sure are. I'd take country bumpkin any day. I love visiting New York City, but I couldn't live here."

"I think I could, but I'd miss the horses and animals," Robert said.

"You do love animals."

"Let's dance." Robert stood up and reached for Sarah's hand. A slow song played in the background. They walked to the dance floor. Robert held Sarah in his arms. They moved rhythmically to the music. Robert loved the smell of the flowery perfume that Sarah was wearing. She turned her head towards Robert. He kissed her lightly on the lips. She lay her head on his shoulder as they danced. He could tell she was tired. "Want to head back to the room?"

"Yes," she said. Robert put his arm around her, and they walked up to their room.

"Should we open the champagne and have some chocolate?"

"I'd love to," Sarah said. Their room had been turned down. Sarah opened the curtains so she could see Times Square. "It is just so exciting to be here."

Robert handed her a glass of champagne. "To us and a lifetime of happiness."

"To us." After drinking their champagne, Sarah went to put on her nightgown in the bathroom. Robert put on his robe. Sarah came out in a gorgeous black nightgown. She looked amazing. The liquor must have taken away her inhibitions because she walked up to him and began kissing him. He was totally turned on but he moved slowly, so as not to not scare Sarah. He took off his robe. They got into bed and he turned off the light. He tenderly made love to Sarah. Twice. He became teary-eyed. The sex was even better than he'd expected. He was so glad she was his wife. He was glad he had made this choice.

Chapter 14

Sarah woke up and gazed at Robert sleeping. He looked so peaceful. It felt wonderful yet odd to be sleeping next to him. She wished she could talk with Brenda about what it was like to have sex. Brenda was still a virgin. She wondered what Brenda was up to. She was afraid to call her sister in case she was angry because she'd eloped.

Sarah got up and used the bathroom. When she came back out Robert was propped on one elbow looking at her. He smiled. She hoped he didn't want sex again. She had to slowly get used to it. They had made love twice last night. It had been better than she expected. She'd only bled a little and it hadn't hurt like she'd thought it would.

"Want to go down and get breakfast? I'm hungry. I can't believe it's almost ten," Sarah said. She walked over to Robert's side of the bed. He turned toward her and pulled her in and kissed her passionately.

"You make me so happy. I'm famished too. You want to shower, or should I?"

"I can if you want," Sarah said. She was surprised that he didn't want sex again. Her friends had told her that when they had got married their husbands constantly wanted sex. "I'll be quick."

"No need to rush, we have all day," Robert said. Why didn't he want sex again? She hoped he found her sexually satisfying. It was tough to know much about sex. People spoke very little about it. Her friends just told her their husbands wanted it all the time. She hoped she would eventually feel more comfortable being naked in front of Robert.

"Wow, you look fantastic," Robert said as she came out of the bathroom. He jumped up, gave Sarah a quick kiss on the check, and went into the bathroom. Sarah went over to the window and looked out over Times Square. She suddenly felt insecure. Why didn't he want sex again? Her friends had told her men loved sex once you were married. She hoped she was good enough for him. Then she thought about her mother. She knew her mother would be angry at her when she got back. Eloping was quite scandalous but Sarah was tired of following the rules. She always followed the rules.

She loved her mother, but she so wanted to be free. Homeschooling had stifled her. Now she could have her own place and live with Robert. She knew her mom had hoped she would go to pharmacy school, but that wasn't a very traditional track for women. Sarah knew that her mom had been an exception by being a one room school teacher and having kids late in life. Sarah wanted children as soon as she could have them. Robert came up behind Sarah and wrapped his arms around her waist.

"This trip is just amazing, Sarah." Robert said. They kissed passionately. It perked her spirits up some.

Sarah and Robert looked out over the water from the top deck as they took the ferry to the Statue of Liberty. It was a gorgeous day. The ferry was absolutely packed with tourists who were out enjoying the city. Sarah looked at Ellis Island. She thought about all the immigrants who must have passed through. Robert put his arm around her. They approached the dock slowly. The ferry rocked as they hit the dock and the crewmen tied up the ferry.

"Wow, does she look amazing," Robert said.

"Who looks amazing?" Sarah asked.

"The Statue of Liberty, silly." Robert pointed. Sarah looked up and laughed. Robert was right; the statue was quite majestic and beautiful with her turquoise copper coating.

"Come on, let's go." Robert grabbed Sarah's hand and pulled her toward the stairwell. Once they got off the boat, Robert put his arm around Sarah. The light breeze that tousled her hair.

"Wow, check out that view," Robert said. He pointed to the New York skyline. It was breathtaking. Sarah's heart leapt. What a perfect day. She loved being with Robert. She was free from her mom.

"Here move over here, let me take a picture of you with the skyline in the background," Robert said.

A gorgeous young blond approached them. "Hi there, we can take your photo if you want. Then you can have a photo with both of you in it." She walked towards Robert and Sarah, a man who must have been her boyfriend walking next to her. Sarah noticed Robert check the woman out. She felt a pang of jealousy.

"That would be great. It's our honeymoon," Robert said. He handed the blond the camera.

"Congratulations, you guys, that's awesome. This is Ned, my fiancé, and I'm Tricia."

"Just push the button here." Robert headed back to Sarah and put his arm around her waist.

"Say cheese," Tricia said. Sarah noticed Tricia was wearing a huge diamond.

"When are you getting married?" Sarah asked Tricia.

"Next summer at the Rockefeller Center. Ned's dad is a

lawyer in the city. Over four hundred people will be invited. I can't wait," Tricia said. She hugged Ned.

"How neat. That must be a lot of planning," Sarah said.

"My mom and Ned's mom are helping me out, so it's been easy. How about you? Where did you get married?"

Sarah was embarrassed. She looked down at her feet then sheepishly over at Robert. "We got married in Maryland. We eloped."

Tricia looked mortified for a second but then composed herself, smiled, and said, "Oh, how nice. Well, have a great honeymoon. Nice to meet you."

Sarah felt miserable inside. She realized she would have to tell people for the rest of her life that she'd eloped. Would everyone think it was a scandal? Why was she feeling so insecure? This wasn't how she'd expected to feel after her wedding.

Chapter 15

"Wow, does the coffee smell good," Dylan said as he walked into the kitchen. Elizabeth was frying bacon. Dylan grabbed a piece and took a bite. "Mom, you make the greatest bacon." He gave her a big hug. *Dylan was the nicest son anyone could ask for,* Elizabeth thought. But Sarah, what on earth was she going to do about Sarah? She'd been gone for several days now. Elizabeth wondered when Sarah would have enough guts to call or stop by after she got back from New York City. She was furious at Robert for eloping with Sarah and furious that his parents and grandparents had helped them out. Elizabeth had never much liked Robert's mother. This made her like her even less. What a scandal.

"How many eggs do you want?" Elizabeth asked as Dylan got a glass out of the cupboard and poured himself some juice.

"I'll take two eggs, Mom." Dylan sat down at the table next to his dad who was reading the newspaper.

"Eugene, put the paper down. Can't you talk more to your kids?" Elizabeth said.

"What are you up to today, Dylan?" Eugene asked as he put the paper down.

"I'm going to help Teddy with the chickens and then his dad's taking us down to the shore to go fishing."

"Well, that sounds like fun," Elizabeth said. Brenda came

in, carrying a beach bag, and grabbed a coffee mug from the cupboard, filling it from the pot on the stove. She took a sip.

"Where are you going?" Dylan asked.

"Down to Hammonasset Beach State Park with Eva Marie, Walter, and her cousin Harry."

"How many eggs do you want?" Elizabeth asked.

"Two," Brenda replied.

"How's Harry? I always liked that young man," Eugene said.

"He likes England a lot and he enjoys the air force. He's been home for about a week. Since today's his last day, we're heading to the beach to get some sun."

"Well, tell him I said hello, and thank him for his service."

"I want to go into the navy someday," Dylan said, buttering his toast.

"You don't want to go in the military, dear. Plus, you need to finish college first," Elizabeth said. She brought Brenda's breakfast over. She worried about Dylan's desire to go into the navy. Dylan had always loved boats and he greatly admired his Uncle Tom who had served in the navy in World War II. He never stopped talking about it. Elizabeth got herself some toast and coffee and sat down with her family. She wondered where Sarah was right now. She missed her even though she was angry at her.

"I have to head downstairs to meet Eva Marie," said Brenda, scraping her plate over the trash can. "She's picking me up in less than five minutes." She picked up her beach bag and headed toward the door.

"Have fun," Elizabeth said. She was happy to see Brenda excited about a man. Brenda worked really hard at her job and at the night courses she was taking. And Elizabeth really liked Eva Marie's family – they were stable, unlike Robert's family. Despite that, Elizabeth had always liked Robert – at least, until he'd eloped with Sarah.

Harry spotted Brenda coming out of the house towards the driveway. *Boy, she looks gorgeous,* he thought. Brenda smiled and waved. It was a perfect day to drive to the shore. Brenda got in the back of the blue convertible with Harry.

"Which way are you going to go?" Harry asked Eva Marie.

"I was just going to go down Route Twenty. Prettier scenery." Eva Marie looked both ways as they headed left onto Main Street.

"Do you get to the beach much in England?" Brenda asked.

"Not too much, plus it's often rainy. It's definitely not as sunny as it is here." Harry noticed how pretty Brenda's hair looked. He loved her beautiful curls and the red lipstick she was wearing. He liked the fact that she knew his family and had had a similar upbringing. He found it hard to meet women that had similar values to himself. He wanted to find someone who wanted a family and that also enjoyed traveling.

"Well, I'm dying to travel the world. I keep saving," Brenda said.

"Where would you go first?"

"I'm not sure. England or France."

"I went to Paris for the weekend once."

"Oh, wow. Did you go up the Eiffel Tower?"

"I did. It was an amazing experience."

"You're so lucky."

"You must be an adventurer. Most women have no desire to travel."

"Well, I totally want to travel," Brenda said. Harry liked her. She had spunk. He noticed Brenda was wearing very stylish sunglasses. He sat back, relaxed, and enjoyed the ride down to Hammonasset. He liked the smell of Brenda's perfume. Eva Marie turned up the radio. They listened to rock songs as they drove.

"Wow, this is glorious." Harry stopped to watch the seagulls overhead.

"You must really enjoy the beach."

"I do, and I've always liked Meigs Point. I like climbing the rocks." Harry stared into Brenda's dark eyes.

"Me too. I'll climb them with you later if you like. I always try to spot crabs." Brenda gazed back at Harry. His heart raced. *A girl who liked climbing rocks,* he thought. So many girls always worried about getting dirty or always looking perfect. He liked Brenda's sense of adventure. They picked a spot on the beach and spread out their blanket and towels. Brenda took off her cover up. She was wearing a red bikini. Harry tried hard not to stare at her.

"Come on, Brenda. Let's go climb the rocks." Harry motioned for her to follow him. As they climbed, Brenda pointed out the crabs that she spotted. The rocks got rougher the farther out they went. At one point Brenda fell back into Harry. Harry instinctively grabbed her as she fell. As he pulled her up, she locked eyes with him. Harry wanted to kiss her then and there, but he controlled himself; he didn't want to scare her off by moving too fast.

"Thanks, Harry." Brenda steadied herself. She leaned in and gave Harry a kiss on the cheek. Harry smiled. He wasn't quite sure what to do next.

"Come on, let's head out to the end." Brenda grabbed his hand. It felt soft and warm. He didn't let go. They slowly climbed out to the end of Meigs Point, hand in hand. When they got to the end they were among a large group of people, many of whom were fishermen. Seagulls were flying above the fishermen who had their lines in the water. It smelled like fish. The rocks were difficult to climb on because they were slippery. Harry slipped and let go of Brenda's hand. He teetered back and forth to keep his balance.

"Don't fall over," Brenda said. Harry steadied himself.

"Hey, can I write you from England? I'd like to keep in touch."

"Of course you can, silly, I'd love it."

Chapter 16

Sarah pulled into the parking lot of the pharmacy. She could see that Laura and Henry were already there. She hoped they didn't know that she'd eloped with Robert – she wanted to tell them herself. Sarah felt happy inside but a little unsettled and insecure. She'd really enjoyed New York City. She and Robert had returned last night to their new apartment. Sarah had some things at the new apartment, but she would eventually have to go to her parents' place to get more of her belongings. She dreaded facing her mother. Laura and Henry looked up as she entered the pharmacy.

"Well, hi there, Miss Sarah, we heard congratulations are in order," Laura said.

"Yeah, congratulations," Henry said.

"Oh, bummer. I wanted to surprise you guys. How did you know?"

"Dylan came down to see if we knew anything as soon as he heard. We're so happy for you and Robert." Laura hugged Sarah.

"Thanks guys. It was wonderful. We got married in Elkton and then spent our honeymoon in New York City. I'll show you some of the pictures later. I better get up front before Gus comes in for his paper." Sarah walked toward the front of the store. She wanted to avoid talking about it. She was confused about the whole thing. She went out the front door and grabbed the bundle of papers and brought them in.

She folded them and put them out on the stand in front of the register. No sooner had she finished than Gus walked in.

"Good morning, Miss Sarah." Gus grabbed a paper and put it on the counter.

"Hi there, Gus. Heading over to the bakery for your coffee?"

"Yes, I am. How was your weekend? I noticed you were gone several days."

"Robert and I got married and went on a honeymoon to New York City." Sarah held up her ring.

"Wow, check that out." Gus looked closely at the ring, "Congratulations!"

"Thanks, Gus. Tell Paula I said hello."

"I will. See you tomorrow." Sarah went over to the boxes behind the counter that had merchandise in them. She needed to price each item and then display them on the shelves. The pharmacy had a large gift and card section. She got her pricing device and started pricing things and putting them out. She loved arranging the gifts and cards. The bell on the front door jingled. It was Mrs. Scott who worked as a nurse in the emergency room at Milltown Hospital in the next town over. Sarah went back up towards the register.

"Hi there, Sarah. Just came in for some cough drops. I've been fighting a cold." Mrs. Scott looked tired.

"No problem, Mrs. Scott, they're right back here. What flavor do you like?"

"Cherry, if you have it."

"Here you go." Sarah handed Mrs. Scott the bag of cherry cough drops.

"Thanks, Sarah. I'm going to grab a candy bar too."

"Okay, I'll meet you up front."

As Sarah was ringing up her items, Mrs. Scott asked, "How's your mom doing?"

"Fine, why do you ask?" Sarah stopped and looked at Mrs. Scott.

"Well, because she was in the emergency room a few days ago." Mrs. Scott handed Sarah a ten dollar bill.

"What? In the hospital?"

"Your mother was in the hospital. You don't remember?" Mrs. Scott gave Sarah a strange look.

"Oh yes, she's doing fine. Sorry. I'm not awake yet today." Sarah handed Mrs. Scott her change. As soon as Mrs. Scott was gone, Sarah headed back to the pharmacy area. She couldn't believe her mom had gone to the hospital. Was it because Sarah had eloped? She hoped her mom was okay. That must mean she was really mad.

"Hey, Laura, did you hear anything about my mom going to the emergency room a couple of days ago?" Sarah asked. Laura looked up from counting out a prescription with a puzzled look.

"No, I didn't hear anything. We just saw Dylan on the afternoon he found out that you'd eloped. I hope she's okay."

"Me too. I'll walk down there on my lunch break to see if she's alright." Sarah felt like a horrible daughter. Her mom had been in the hospital and she hadn't even known.

Hazel walked into the pharmacy for her shift. She'd worked at the pharmacy since Henry and Laura had opened it. People often described her as a 'firecracker in a bottle' because she was high energy and lots of fun. Sarah loved Hazel.

"Well, hi there, Miss Sarah. I heard you got hitched last week. Congratulations." Hazel came behind the counter and gave Sarah a hug.

"Well, thank you, Hazel." Sarah said.

"I still remember the day I married Tom. Happiest day of my life. You'll love married life. There's nothing better. I better go put my stuff in the back."

Sarah walked back to the soda fountain to get it ready for the lunch rush. Lots of high school students came in at lunch time for milkshakes and BLTs. She opened up bacon and put the strips in the pan. She turned on the burners. The smell of bacon spread throughout the store. Sarah was getting hungry. She kept thinking about her mom. Was she okay? Was she mad at her? She would bring her a BLT when she got to take her break. Her mom loved the pharmacy's BLTs. Maybe it could be a peace offering.

Chapter 17

Elizabeth and her sister-in-law, Abbey, sat at the kitchen table drinking tea and playing a game of rummy. Abbey was married to Eugene's brother Joe, who owned the German bakery on Main Street. Joe had taken over the family bakery when their dad retired. The bakery was a popular spot for donuts, black and white cookies, bread, and rolls. Elizabeth loved Abbey dearly. They had become good friends when Elizabeth started dating Eugene. Elizabeth had met Eugene when she'd moved to Laurelville from Virginia to conduct psychological testing of adolescent females at Lilac Lane, a juvenile detention facility for girls. Before that she'd been a one-room school teacher in Virginia. She rented a place across the street from where Eugene's family lived. Eugene was an architect for a local company.

Elizabeth always said hello to Eugene when she saw him on the street. One day he came over to her when she was leaving for work. He asked her if she wanted to have dinner with him. Elizabeth said yes and the rest was history. Elizabeth admired Eugene's intelligence and thoughtfulness. He was tall and handsome as well.

Elizabeth married Eugene when she was thirty-two years old. Thirty-two was considered old to get married back then. Many had thought Elizabeth would be an old maid for the rest of her life, but Elizabeth knew she was just waiting for the right person. Elizabeth was the serious intellectual type and she had had her own career, unusual for women.

"Rummy," Abbey suddenly shouted and slapped her cards down.

"You just keep winning, Abbey," Elizabeth said. She took a sip of her tea.

"You heard anything from Sarah?" Abbey asked.

"Not a word. I don't know what has gotten into her," Elizabeth said.

"Well, at least Robert is a decent person. I thought you liked him. He's always pleasant enough." Abbey took a bite of her sandwich.

"I know, but she's too young to get married. She's only twenty." Elizabeth gathered the cards and shuffled them.

"You know my girls married young too. They're happy."

"I know. I'm trying to be open-minded. I just wish she'd spent more time working on a degree for a career." Elizabeth put the deck down and turned a card over to start the discard pile.

"Well, she is taking classes at night, isn't she?"

"Yes. Let's hope she keeps that up." Elizabeth picked a card from the deck and discarded one.

"I bet she will. Isn't she almost done?"

"Yes, just the class this semester and one next semester. I just wonder if I sheltered them too much by home schooling them through high school."

"Why do you think that? They were really involved in community and church activities."

"You're right, but I just think she rushed into this marriage. I have a bad feeling about it." Elizabeth poured each of them more tea. Abbey often came by after working an early morning shift at the bakery. She and Joe were planning on retiring soon. They were selling the bakery to a nice couple from Maine who were moving to Connecticut to be near their grandchildren. Elizabeth had stopped working when she had her three children. She missed working but raising three children and homeschooling them was a lot of work.

"You looking forward to retiring?" Elizabeth asked.

"Yes, Joe wants to travel and spend a couple of months a year in Sarasota. You'll have to come visit us." Abbey put down a card.

"I'd love to. I wish Eugene and I traveled more." Elizabeth added sugar to her cup of tea and stirred. She heard the front door open. She wondered who on earth would be coming home at this time of day. She looked up and there was Sarah, carrying a small brown paper bag. Elizabeth was shocked that Sarah had the guts to show up after what she'd done.

"Sarah, congratulations, my dear," Abbey ran over to Sarah and gave her a big hug.

"Thanks, Aunt Abbey. Great to see you." Sarah hugged her aunt tight. Elizabeth didn't move. Abbey let go of Sarah and sat back down. There was an awkward silence.

"I brought you a BLT just the way you like it, Mom." Sarah put the bag down on the table.

"I already ate," Elizabeth said coldly. Abbey gave Elizabeth an uncomfortable look.

"Can I have half?" Abbey asked. "I'm actually still hungry."

"You can have it all." Elizabeth stared at Sarah. Abbey opened the bag, took out the sandwich, and unwrapped it. She took a bite.

"I'm sorry, Mama. I know you're angry that I eloped." Sarah shifted nervously on her feet.

"Are you pregnant?"

Abbey choked on a piece of sandwich. She grabbed her tea and drank it fast.

"Pregnant? Me? Is that what you think?"

"Everyone in town thinks that," Elizabeth said. Abbey gave Elizabeth another shocked look.

"I'm not pregnant. I love Robert and wanted to marry him and you wouldn't even let me wear my engagement ring." Sarah looked as if she was going to cry.

"Wow, look at the time. I better head off. Thanks Elizabeth for lunch and the tea. Thanks Sarah for the BLT, and congratulations again." Abbey jumped up and kissed Elizabeth on the cheek. She then kissed Sarah and hurried out the front door.

"Now you drove off Abbey. What next? What is wrong with you?" Elizabeth asked.

"Nothing, Mama. I came to see how you were. Mrs. Scott told me you were in the emergency room last week."

"I'm fine. My heart just acted up some. Don't worry about me." Elizabeth stood up and brought the dirty plates to the sink.

"Will you come by and see our place sometime soon? We rented a place above the package store on the river," Sarah said.

"No. I don't want to see Robert ever again. He never even asked your father's permission to marry you. You eloped. Do you know how scandalous that is? Plus, Robert should have known you're too young to get married. I can't believe his family helped you. That mother of his is trouble too. I never liked her. You can come by anytime and visit but he can't."

Sarah started crying. Elizabeth continued working at the sink, ignoring her.

"I can't believe you're going to be this way. Robert is my husband."

"I'm not the one behaving badly. You are. Now please get out of here. You're upsetting me even more."

"Mom, please." Sarah's heart felt broken.

"Get out of here. Now. You can come back another time. I just need some space."

Sarah walked out of the front door. What had she done?

Chapter 18

Robert was cooking dinner. He was so happy that he and Sarah now had a place of their own. He loved it. Sarah was his best friend and made him content with his life. He didn't miss living with his family. His mother could be so domineering if she drank too much. He went to the cupboard and took out plates and placed them on the table. He then got napkins and silverware and set the table. He lit a cinnamon-scented candle that he had placed on the middle of the table. Sarah rushed through the door.

"Hey there, sweetie." Robert moved toward Sarah to give her a hug. Sarah embraced him and put her head on his shoulder.

"Oh, Robert, I had such a bad day. Mom and I had a fight. She refuses to come see our new place. She says I can visit her but you can't. She's so stubborn." She moved away. Robert hoped she'd notice the set table and candle, but she didn't. It hurts his feelings. She was too focused on her mother. Why couldn't she just be happy?

"I can't believe her. She loves you, Robert. Why is she doing this?" Sarah poured herself a glass of water.

"She'll come around. You know she thought we were too young to get married." Robert went to the stove and picked up the frying pan with the pork chops and walked over and put one on each plate.

"Wow, Robert, thanks so much for making this wonderful

dinner," Sarah said. Robert was glad that she'd finally noticed. Sarah seemed so distracted. He hoped her mother would get over the fact they eloped. It was considered scandalous. But Robert didn't care, he was just so glad he and Sarah could be together. He thought about going and apologizing to her mother, but he didn't know how she would react.

After they finished eating they walked over to the river.

"What a beautiful night," Sarah said.

"It sure is. You look gorgeous too." Robert squeezed Sarah's hand and she blushed. Robert couldn't wait until later after dancing at the studio. He wanted sex badly. They walked peacefully hand in hand, passing couples and families as they went.

Suddenly Sarah stopped and pointed. "Hey, isn't that Gary from church? Over there, walking with another man?"

Robert looked over and sure enough it was Gary. Robert wondered why Gary was even here since he lived in the next town over. He hoped Gary wasn't going to make trouble.

"Shouldn't we go say hi?" Sarah asked.

"No. They look busy. Let's keep walking," Robert tugged at Sarah's arm.

"Okay, okay. You don't have to pull my arm off," Sarah said. Gary saw Robert and gave a slight wave. Luckily Sarah didn't see it. Robert ignored him and quickly turned to walk the other way.

"Hey, why are you turning around?" Sarah asked.

"Look at the time. We better head over to the dance studio," Robert said. He pointed to his watch. Sarah followed him. Robert looked over his shoulder to make sure Gary wasn't following them. He was headed in the other direction with the man he was with. Robert had thought that once he married Sarah that the other part of his life would go away. It wasn't going to be as easy as he'd thought. He sighed.

"What's wrong?" Sarah asked.

"Oh nothing. Just want to go practice dancing since we're competing in a few weeks at the biggest fair in Connecticut. Guess I'm a little nervous."

"I know. I am too, but I love dancing with you." She stopped outside their apartment and gave Robert a kiss. It calmed him down. He sure hoped Gary would stay away from them. Robert was glad that Sarah was naïve and had never suspected anything about him and Gary. He wanted it to stay that way. He needed the stability of Sarah. He loved her.

"You sure are the love of my life," Robert said. "Let me go grab the car keys and we can head off."

As they drove to the dance studio, Sarah said, "Brenda's hot on Harry, Eva Marie's cousin. She called me today on her break to tell me while I was at the pharmacy. First, she yelled at me for eloping and then she jumped to telling me about Harry."

"No way. When did that happen? I thought he was overseas."

"He came back on break when we were in New York City."

"Well, I always liked Harry. Good for her, but that sure is a long-distance relationship." Robert pulled into the parking lot of the dance studio.

"Brenda probably likes the romance and drama of it all. Dating a military man based in England. Maybe she's just jealous because we got married. She's always wanted to travel the world though. Maybe that's part of Harry's appeal."

"Well, I wouldn't want to have a long-distance relationship." Robert said.

Chapter 19

Eva Marie jumped when Brenda came running through the door. She dropped the candy bars she'd been holding. "Brenda, what on earth is wrong with you? You scared the dickens out of me."

Brenda waved a letter in the air. "I got another letter in the mail from Harry. I can't believe it's been almost two months since I saw him. Guess what? He says your parents and his parents are going to England in a few months and they're going to ask my mom if I can go too. I'm not supposed to know yet. Wouldn't that be awesome?"

"I heard them talking about it but when they realized I was listening they changed the subject. I think they didn't want you to find out until they asked your mother." Eva Marie bent down to pick up the candy bars.

"England. How cool. I've always wanted to go overseas." Brenda sat down in a chair behind the cash register.

"I've always wanted to go too, but it's so expensive. How can you afford it?"

"He's paying for the ticket!"

"For real? Man, he must really like you."

"Well, I sure like him."

"Why do you like him so much?" Eva Marie asked.

"Well, he's handsome. He likes to travel. He would make beautiful babies."

"That's true," Eva Marie said. "He is my cousin after all. Good looks run in the family." They both laughed.

"And I like that he's brave and serving the country. He's smart and fun. Did I say he likes to travel? I want to travel."

"When are they going to ask your mom?" Eva Marie asked.

"Sometime in the next week. Before they ask her, Harry wanted to make sure that I wanted to go."

"You really think your mom might let you go? Look at what she did to Sarah. Hey, is she talking to Sarah yet?"

"Barely. It's been almost two months now and my mom won't budge. She says Robert isn't allowed over at our house and she won't go to their apartment. Mom only sees Sarah if she stops by alone."

"That is a bummer."

"It sure is. But why on earth did she go and elope? I think the whole town thought she was pregnant." Brenda stuck out her stomach and put her hands on it.

"Stop it, Brenda. You're being mean," Eva Marie replied.

"Well then, she eloped because she's afraid of Mama."

Eva Marie's mom, Giovanna, walked through the back door of the shop. She was carrying a medium-sized cardboard box filled with items for sale. She came in and put the box and her purse on the counter.

"Well, hey there girls. How's the day been?"

"Slow, slow, slow," Eva Marie replied.

"Wonder why. What were you two talking about when I walked in?"

"I was asking if Elizabeth had made peace with Sarah yet."

"Has she?"

"No. Robert still can't come to our house and Mama refuses to go see her apartment. She just thinks Sarah was too young to marry Robert."

"She'll come around one day. Your mom always seemed

to liked Robert. The elopement was tough on her. It would be tough on any mom. Doesn't look good for the family. But everyone knows you have a good family. Also, I think people are glad Robert was able to find Sarah and create a life away from his mom."

"That's true. Robert's had a very difficult childhood. Yet he rose above it. He's done okay," Brenda said.

"Robert's a good person. He'll make Sarah happy. Your mom should get over the elopement soon. If she doesn't, do you think maybe there's some other reason she's mad about the marriage?"

"Not that I know of. That is a good question though. I'll ask her."

Chapter 20

Sarah and Robert walked down to the parking lot. Sarah carried a banana cream pie. It was Robert's favorite. The river sparkled in the afternoon. There were lots of cars parked across the street in the park. Families and couples were walking by the river.

"I think it's so nice Henry and Laura invited us over for dinner," Robert said.

"It sure is." Sarah looked up at Robert as he closed the door. He leaned in and gave her a kiss. They drove through their beautiful country town. He thought Sarah was being unusually quiet.

"Anything bothering you, sweetheart?" Robert put his hand on top of hers.

"Just tired, that's all. Have been feeling a little queasy today."

"Did you eat something bad?'

"I don't think so, maybe I just caught a bug." Sarah patted her stomach. Robert pulled into Henry and Laura's driveway. Henry and Laura owned a large white colonial house on ten acres of land. They had their own pond and beautiful gardens. They even had a pasture with sheep. As Robert got closer to the house, he noticed lots of cars parked at the side.

"You didn't say there were others coming besides us, Sarah. What's going on?"

"I have no idea, Robert." Sarah looked at all the cars in

amazement. Suddenly she saw Dylan, Brenda, Heather and others come streaming out of the house towards their car.

"Surprise, surprise, congratulations newlyweds!"

Robert saw Sarah's eyes welling up with tears. He thought she looked beautiful.

"Sarah, why are you crying?"

"I don't know. I'm overwhelmed."

"Congratulations, sis." Dylan grabbed Sarah's hand and pulled her from the car. Robert watched Dylan pin a corsage on Sarah and kiss her on the cheek. Brenda was taking photos as he did. Robert smiled. His door suddenly opened.

"Come on out here. Your turn." Heather motioned for Robert to get out of the car. Hazel, Heather, and Robert's parents watched. Robert's mom, Mary, gave him a big hug while his dad slapped him on the back. When Robert's mom pulled back, Heather came up with a boutonniere for him.

"I'm so happy for you guys," Heather said as she pinned it on. Brenda came over to take a photo.

"Let's go in the house, everyone's waiting."

Robert watched Sarah; she was radiating happiness. She was beaming. As they walked into the house, people came up and hugged and congratulated them. It seemed like the whole town was in Henry and Laura's house.

"Welcome, welcome." Laura moved forward from the back of the crowd.

"Oh Laura, you shouldn't have done this." Sarah embraced her.

"Of course I should. I'm so happy for you both." Laura turned to Robert and hugged him too.

"Welcome newlyweds. Sorry it took us so long to get this party together. Come on back and let me get you guys a drink." Henry motioned them to follow him. Robert noticed Sarah's eyes scanning the crowd. He figured she was looking for her mother. Robert did spot her aunt and uncle,

Abbey and Joe. Eva Marie and her parents were there as well. Suddenly he saw Sarah's dad Eugene walk in from the back yard. His heart leaped with excitement. Robert waited to see if Elizabeth would follow, but Eugene shut the door behind him. Robert's heart sank. His eyes met Sarah's; he could sense her disappointment. He smiled at her. He and Sarah stopped and greeted people as they followed Henry through the house. Eventually they made it to the bar area off of the living room.

"What can I get you?" Henry asked.

"Just ginger ale for me if you have it." Sarah put her hand on the edge of the bar.

"Of course, how about you, Robert?"

"I'll take a gin and tonic." Robert put his arm around Sarah. He noticed glasses of champagne on the table behind Henry. Henry handed Robert his drink.

"Okay, now that the guests of honor are here and settled," Henry called, "let's eat. The food is out in the back yard. There's plenty. Sarah and Robert, you guys go first."

Robert followed Sarah out into the back yard. Strings of white, red, and blue lights hung around the patio area. It looked magical. Robert leaned in and kissed Sarah. He was so happy. He spotted his mom, drinking a glass of wine. He hoped she wouldn't drink too much and embarrass herself and him.

Robert's mom had had a life full of turmoil. Her dad had been a womanizer. Her two brothers had drowned when her dad was supposed to be watching them. He'd had a woman inside the house with him. Robert's mother had never gotten over the death of her two brothers. It haunted her. She'd been off at a friend's house when it happened. Robert sensed that she in some way blamed herself for their deaths. He figured that was what drove his mom's drinking. Unfortunately, her drinking had ruined his childhood, and that of his siblings.

Robert was the oldest so he bore most of his mother's verbal abuse. He tried throughout his childhood to protect his younger siblings.

His brother Raymond, who lived in Vermont, didn't hang out at home much as a teen. He spent a lot of time at their aunt's house in Laurelville. He was naturally bright and worked hard. He got a scholarship to the University of Connecticut to study engineering. He was doing well as an engineer. Robert's sister, Violet, was sent to England to live with relatives and attend a private high school. The family wanted her to be protected.

Sarah put her arm around Robert's waist which startled him. "Oops, sorry, let me grab a plate."

"You were off in space somewhere," Sarah said. The food looked fantastic. It was quite the spread. Lasagna, eggplant parmesan, chicken parmesan meatballs, sausage and onions, ziti, garlic bread, antipasto salad. Margo's, a locally-owned family Italian restaurant, had catered for the event.

"Wow, this looks so good," Sarah said. She placed a spoonful of food onto her plate.

"Sure does." Robert grabbed a napkin and silverware. He headed over to a table on the patio and sat down with his food. Sarah followed. Dylan, Heather, Brenda, and Eugene joined them.

"Sorry your mom didn't come, Sarah. She is stubborn. Robert, she really likes you. She just didn't want Sarah to get married so young." Eugene put his plate down.

"I know. It's okay. I'm glad you all came." Robert put his hand on Eugene's arm. Robert took a bite of food and watched his mom and dad go over to a table across the yard. His mom had gotten another glass of wine. He sure hoped that was her last drink. She embarrassed him when she drank too much. She became loud and obnoxious. It tormented him. Why couldn't he have a normal mother? He didn't even know if his mother loved him. At least he knew his father did.

"Hi, Robert. You look like you are in outer space," Dylan said. Robert snapped out of it and looked at Dylan. Dylan always made Robert feel good. That's part of why Robert loved Sarah so much. He enjoyed feeling part of her family since his own childhood had been so unstable.

"Dylan, I guess you like garlic bread," Robert said when he saw how much Dylan had on his plate.

"I'm a growing man," Dylan said. Heather smiled widely at Dylan. Robert wondered if Heather had a crush on him. He thought Heather would be good for Dylan. She was as nice as Dylan was. Henry came around with the tray of champagne. After everyone took a glass, Henry and Laura moved toward Robert and Sarah.

"Everyone, everyone. May I have your attention." Henry banged a knife against his champagne glass.

"We want to let you know how happy we are that all of you could come celebrate the marriage of Sarah and Robert. We've watched their romance blossom over time at the pharmacy. We always had to keep plenty of butterscotch topping on hand because Robert ate more butterscotch sundaes than I could count." Everyone laughed. Robert blushed. Sarah pressed his hand.

"We want to celebrate their love today and the beginning of their life together. Sarah and Robert, we love you." Laura welled up with tears. Everyone raised their glasses and then sipped their champagne.

"Now, you two need to follow Brenda so you can help us all get some dessert," Laura said. Brenda moved across the yard to a table set up in the back next to a fountain.

"Everyone come around," Brenda called to the crowd. Robert and Sarah followed Brenda. Robert spotted a large sheet cake with vanilla frosting. On it was a soda fountain counter with hearts decorated with frosting. The words *Congratulations Robert and Sarah* were written above it.

"That is amazing," Sarah said.

"Aunt Abbey and Uncle Joe made it. They loved designing it," Brenda said. "Go over there behind the cake and hold it at an angle. I want to get a nice picture of you."

Laura came over with a knife and handed it to Sarah. "You need to cut the first piece together."

Sarah took the knife and Robert put his hand on top of hers. They slowly cut the first piece of cake and put it on one of the pretty paper plates.

"Now you need to feed Robert some, sis," Dylan said. Sarah grabbed a piece of cake and neatly placed some in Robert's mouth. Everyone laughed. Robert then grabbed a piece and put it in Sarah's mouth.

"You guys are too neat. Hey, cut me a piece," Dylan said.

"There's coffee in the kitchen everyone," Laura said as she handed out cake. Robert noticed that his mom took some cake. But instead of going to get coffee she went over to the bar area and poured herself another glass of wine. Why couldn't Sarah's mom have come to the party and his mom stayed home? Life was full of contradictions. Sometimes he just wished his mom would disappear or move to another town.

Chapter 21

Elizabeth walked down Main Street to Laurelville's Variety Store. Eva Marie's mom Giovanna had called the day before and asked Elizabeth if she could stop by the store sometime this week. Giovanna said she had to ask Elizabeth something. Elizabeth wondered what it might be. She liked Giovanna because she was an independent woman who owned her own business with her husband. Elizabeth valued work. She wished Sarah had gone to pharmacy school.

Elizabeth enjoyed living on Main Street. She loved the old style colonial homes. It was lovely that everyone in the town knew one another and helped each other out. It was still a big farming community. The sun was shining, and the birds were out in full force, dancing between the old oak trees.

"I'm so happy that you came by," said Giovanna as Elizabeth walked into the store.

"No problem at all. It's nice to be out on such a gorgeous day."

"Well, I wanted to talk with you about something important. As you know, Brenda has been writing to Harry."

"I know. She's always checking the mail for his letters and he calls at least once a week."

"Well, Anthony and I are going to England in two months

with Harry's parents to visit him. I wondered if Brenda could possibly join us. Harry has offered to pay for her ticket."

"Are you serious? I'm stunned."

"I've already looked into it and Brenda can stay on the base at a nice woman's home. We'll be right down the road in a hotel we've stayed in before. She can fly with us. We'll be gone for about ten days. Harry is a good boy and a gentleman. As you know, he has a degree in engineering."

"Yes, yes, I've always liked Harry. He has a good head on his shoulders. Could I think about this? Does Brenda know?"

"We haven't said anything to her, but I can't guarantee that Harry hasn't. I told him not to mention it until I talked with you, but you know youth." The bell rang and the front door of the store opened. Mrs. Clark from down the road walked in and headed down one of aisles.

"Well, let me think about it."

"That would be marvelous." Giovanna went to the cash register to serve Mrs. Clark.

"Thanks Giovanna, have a wonderful day and talk to you soon." Elizabeth headed down Main Street. *Guess my daughters are both now in romantic relationships,* she thought. Brenda was four years older than Sarah and she would be chaperoned. And Elizabeth liked Harry quite a bit. She liked Robert too but she just didn't think he was right for Sarah. And Sarah was so young. Elizabeth decided she would drive over and see Abbey at the bakery. She needed some advice.

As Elizabeth walked towards the bakery she could smell fresh bread. People went there from all the surrounding towns to get their bread and sandwich rolls. Elizabeth would come every Sunday after church to get rolls so the family could have cold cut sandwiches. The bakery was crowded but Abbey spotted Elizabeth right away.

"Well, hey there, Elizabeth, what a surprise. I'll be with you as soon as the line dies down. Why don't you go in the back and find Joe?" Abbey wrapped a sandwich in white paper.

"Hi there, Joe," Elizabeth said as she walked into the baking area.

"Elizabeth, nice to see you. How are you?" Joe took a pan of rolls out of the oven.

"I'm doing well. Here let me help you." Elizabeth grabbed an apron from a hook and put it on. "What can I do?"

"Feel like frosting some donuts? They're over there and the chocolate icing is right next to them."

"I'd be happy to. I swear Joe you work in the best smelling environment of anyone I know." Elizabeth grabbed a spatula and began to frost. Joe laughed.

"How's Eugene doing? I heard he was working on some big design project." Joe took another tray out of the oven.

"Yeah, he's been super busy, but he loves it. Guess who's been asked to go to England?"

"Are you going to meet the queen?"

"No, not me. Brenda's been invited to go with the Rigoni family to visit Harry in a couple of months. She's quite infatuated."

"Infatuated with who?" Abbey asked as she walked in.

"Brenda has the hots for Harry," Joe said.

"Joe." Elizabeth shook her head.

"Brenda's been invited to go to England in a couple of months with the Rigoni family to see Harry," Joe said.

"She'll be chaperoned. What do you think?" Elizabeth looked at Abbey.

"Well, I think that's a great opportunity for Brenda. She's always talked about wanting to travel the world. Harry's a

great guy and he's from a good family. You should let her go."
Abbey grabbed a tray of rolls and walked back to the front
of the bakery.

"That was a quick answer. She's usually not quite that
fast." Joe turned the oven off.

"You're right, Joe. I guess that means I need to let Brenda
go." Elizabeth put her finger in the frosting bowl, licked it
and smiled.

Chapter 22

*S*arah was frustrated. She couldn't believe her mother still wouldn't let Robert visit the house, and still wouldn't visit their apartment either. Her mom had deeply hurt her feelings by not coming to the party that Laura and Henry had held to celebrate her marriage to Robert. She couldn't figure out why her mother had turned against Robert. Eloping wasn't such a terrible thing to do if you loved someone. *Okay, I need to pull myself together,* she thought.

There were two police cars out front at the pharmacy. The police did stop by every now and then but she'd never seen two cars there at once. *Oh no,* she thought, *I hope the store hasn't been robbed.* She wasn't sure whether to go in but just then an officer came out. It was Patrick, a good friend of her family.

"Hi, Patrick. Is everything okay?"

"Hi, Sarah. We had a complaint. I can't talk about it but I'm sure Henry will when he's ready. You might not want to bring it up right now. Give your parents my regards."

"I'll do that, Patrick. Take care." Inside there were two policemen in the back talking with Henry and Laura. Hazel was at the front register and she motioned for Sarah to come over.

"Did you hear what happened?"

"No. I saw Patrick outside, but he didn't tell me anything."

"All this drama," said Heather, joining them.

"Will someone tell me what's going on?" Sarah said.

"Apparently someone got the wrong medication a month ago. The family originally thought the person had gotten really sick because of their illness but now they think it's because of a medication error. They tied it to this pharmacy. I don't know the details. I heard them talking back there. I don't even know which patient or anything. The police are in the pharmacy area looking through the files. One of the policemen brought in a vial with a label on it in a bag. It must be evidence. This could be bad for the pharmacy. I heard them talking about getting a lawyer involved too. Oops, here comes a customer; we better stop talking about this now."

"How's your mother been?" Heather asked.

"She still says she never wants to see Robert again."

"It'll get better, kid. Just give her time. She'll come around." Hazel put her arm around Sarah.

"You don't know my mom. She's one stubborn woman."

"Guess it runs in the family." Hazel winked at Sarah. "Come on, let's unpack the stock and keep out of the way while the cops are back there."

They tried their best to look busy and to ignore what was going on in the back of the pharmacy. They unpacked greeting cards, make-up, glass figurines, and t-shirts. No customers came in as they worked, until lunchtime when some students came in.

"Milkshake time." Heather stood up and walked over to the soda fountain area. About five high school students were sitting on the stools there. "Hi guys, what can I make you today?"

"Hi, Heather. I'll take a chocolate shake," one of the boys said. Sarah walked over to help Heather. When the high school let out, the soda fountain got very busy.

"I'll have strawberry."

"Vanilla for me."

"Chocolate for me."

"Root beer float for me. Heather, what's going on back there?" Ginny pointed towards the pharmacy area.

"Yeah, why are there cop cars outside?" Tommy asked.

"I'm not quite sure. We're trying to give them privacy back there." Heather scooped out strawberry ice cream into a large cup.

"You think it was a robbery?" Ginny asked.

"No, definitely not a robbery." Heather poured root beer into a glass and added a scoop of vanilla ice cream. Sarah scooped out ice cream for the chocolate shakes. The door swung open and Dylan walked in. Sarah noticed that Heather suddenly dropped the spoon she was using and glanced at Dylan. Sarah wondered if Heather liked Dylan. *No, it couldn't be,* she thought.

"Hi there, sis." Sarah wrapped her arms around her brother. Heather watched and smiled. Dylan winked at Heather and sat down on the only stool that was left at the soda fountain.

"Hi, Dylan," one of the young women sitting at the soda fountain said. Dylan ignored her and looked at Heather.

"Hey, Heather. How are your classes going at Laurelville?"

"Great. I'm actually enjoying my advanced chemistry course. How are your classes?" Heather scooped ice cream into a cup.

"It's all going great. I can't believe I'm almost done with my third year. Doesn't it just speed by?"

"Sure does. What can I get you?" Heather came over to Dylan and leaned in close to him, blocking the other girl sitting at the counter who was eyeing Dylan.

"I'll just take a Coke. You look nice today," Dylan said. *Hmm... maybe he likes Heather,* Sarah thought.

Henry walked over and motioned for Sarah to follow him back to the pharmacy area. The policemen had left. Henry looked stressed. Sarah followed him into the office where Laura was sitting, sobbing.

"Laura, what's wrong?"

"A major mistake was made on a prescription. Quinidine was filled for Quinine. Quinine is for leg cramps and Quinidine for the heart. It is very dangerous for someone to be on Quinidine who shouldn't be." Henry sat down next to Laura and put his hand on her knee.

"Oh no." Sarah felt sick. She didn't know if she should ask who'd made the mistake.

"It was Mrs. Miller. I feel so bad."

"Oh no. Is she okay?" Sarah started tearing up herself. Mrs. Miller was a local teacher who was loved by everyone in town.

"She's in the hospital. We can't give you too many details. We've talked with our lawyer and are cooperating with police. Best to not talk about it. The story most likely will make it into the newspapers. We wanted to tell each of you one by one."

"Can I ask who made the error?"

"We're not a hundred per cent sure yet, so we can't discuss it. We have an idea but the detectives need to talk to different people first," Henry said.

"Okay, thanks for letting me know."

"Can you cover the soda fountain while I tell Heather?" Henry asked.

"Sure," Sarah said as she thought about what a bad day this had turned out to be. But her ongoing disagreement with her mother seemed like nothing compared to the investigation going on at the pharmacy.

Chapter 23

Elizabeth sat at the table peeling the skin off of the peaches that she was going to can. She was still annoyed at Sarah. Why did she keep pushing for Robert to come over? Nothing good would come from it. Elizabeth needed to tell Eugene about Brenda going to England. She hoped he'd be okay about it.

The front door opened and in walked Eugene. "Elizabeth, where are you?"

"Back here, canning peaches. I baked you a peach pie," Elizabeth called. Eugene walked into the kitchen and gave her a kiss on the lips.

"How was work?" Elizabeth asked.

"It was good. We had a big lunch meeting with a new client and it went really well. Looks like we'll be building a new elementary school for Robinsville." Eugene grabbed a piece of peach pie and put it on a plate. He sat down at the table with Elizabeth.

"Well, that sounds like fun."

"How was your day?"

"It was good. I went over to the orchards today to get the peaches. Then Sarah came over for lunch. I decided to can the peaches after making the pie. I'm almost done."

"Why don't you have a piece of pie with me? I'll pour us some milk." Eugene got up and went over to the cupboard and took out two tall glasses. He poured them each a glass of milk while Elizabeth cut herself a piece of pie.

"Wow, this is so good. It's still warm. Thank you for making this. Hey, are you and Sarah getting along better?"

"We get along just fine until she brings up me letting Robert come over or us going over there. Why can't she leave it alone?"

"You have to get over it sooner or later. You can't be mad at her forever. Sure she's young but we can't change what she did. Plus, you always liked Robert."

"Yes, but that still doesn't mean I think that Sarah should have married him."

"Well, it isn't normal to not see your daughter's new husband. You're being stubborn. Give them a chance."

"I just don't think he's the right person for her and I can't believe she eloped. They're both only twenty. But anyway, I have something else to tell you."

"What's that, my dear?"

"Well, Mrs. Rigoni asked me if Brenda could go with them and Harry's parents to see Harry in England in a couple of months." Elizabeth watched to see his reaction.

"I know that." Eugene stood up and cut himself another piece of pie.

"You know about it? How do you know about it?"

"Joe told me." Eugene sat down.

"When did he tell you that?"

"Today. He called me at work about something else and then he told me how neat it was that Brenda was going to England."

"Are you okay with it?"

"I sure am. Harry's a great guy, serving our country and all. He comes from a good family. What more could we ask for?"

"Are you worried at all about her traveling all that way?"

"Not at all. Brenda's always had a wild side. She craves adventure. What's more adventurous then flying to England to see a guy in the air force?"

"I guess you're right. Plus, she'll be with a bunch of adults."

"Exactly. Not a lot of hanky panky can happen with all of them around."

"Eugene," Elizabeth said.

"Have you talked with Brenda about it yet?"

"No, I guess I might as well do it when she gets home. She should be here any minute." Elizabeth stood up and took her plate and glass over to the sink, then sat down and carried on peeling peaches. Eugene grabbed a knife and started helping. The door opened and Brenda came in.

"Wow, it smells incredible in here. You two look busy," Brenda said. She opened the refrigerator and took out a bottle of Fresca.

"Have a piece of pie if you want," Elizabeth said.

"You bet I will. Nobody makes a pie as good as you, Mom." Brenda cut herself a piece and then sat down with Eugene and Elizabeth.

"Brenda, we need to talk with you about something," Elizabeth said.

"What's that?"

"Well, Mrs. Rigoni," Elizabeth started but stopped when Brenda jumped up from the table.

"Wow. Did she finally ask you guys? Can I go? Can I go?" Brenda was beaming.

"Are you sure you want to go? It's a long trip," Eugene said.

"Oh, I so want to go. I really like Harry and you know I've always wanted to travel the world. Please, please can I go?"

"They've arranged for you to stay at Mrs. Singer's house. She lives on the base. Her husband is in the military. She rents rooms to women who come to visit from the United States. Are you okay with all that? You need to act respectable," Elizabeth said.

"Yeah, yeah, I know. It's fine. You know I'll behave. Plus, I'll be with all of Harry's family." Brenda grasped Elizabeth's hands and stared at her, waiting for an answer.

"Okay, you can go," Elizabeth said. Brenda leaned in and gave her mom a big hug and then kissed her dad on the cheek.

"You've made me so happy. I can't believe it. I'm going to England!"

Chapter 24

Dylan grabbed the newspaper off the front stoop. He checked the headlines as he walked back into the house. There was a picture of the town's pharmacy on the front with the headline 'Bad Medication Error Made at Local Pharmacy.' He quickly skimmed the article. "Holy cow," Dylan said to himself as he turned and ran up the stairs.

"Mom, Mom, check this out." Dylan threw the paper down on the kitchen table where Elizabeth was sitting and drinking coffee. "Did you know about this? It's Mrs. Miller. The police were there the other day but no one knew why."

Elizabeth picked up the newspaper. Dylan poured himself some coffee while Elizabeth read the article. Eugene walked into the kitchen. "Dylan, what's all the excitement this morning?"

"Someone at the pharmacy made a mistake and Mrs. Miller got sick. She almost died. It's in this morning's paper." Dylan sat down at the table.

"How sad this is?" Elizabeth handed the newspaper to Eugene.

"You know, Mrs. Miller hasn't been back to work at the high school. They've had a substitute. Someone told me they hope she gets better enough to hopefully go back to work in a few weeks. Mrs. Miller is one of the best teachers." Dylan took a sip of his coffee.

"Wonder if Sarah knows about this?" Elizabeth said.

"She was there yesterday when the police were there," Dylan said.

"It doesn't say who made the mistake, does it?" Elizabeth asked.

"No. Why?" Dylan asked.

"Doesn't Sarah sometimes help in the pharmacy?"

"Sometimes, but not that often. Just like everyone else."

"This is awful for Laura and Henry. They've been served with a subpoena and are being sued by the Miller family. How tragic this is for everyone involved." Eugene sat down. Brenda walked into the kitchen.

"Why do you all look so gloomy?"

"Turns out that Mrs. Miller is really sick because of an error made at the pharmacy." Elizabeth wiped tears from her eyes. Brenda grabbed the paper.

"Well, have any of you called Sarah and asked her about it?"

"No," Dylan replied.

"What's wrong with you guys?" Brenda picked up the phone and dialed.

"Oh, hey there, Robert. I'm fine. Can I talk to Sarah a second? Hi, Sarah. What on earth's going on at the pharmacy? Did you see the newspaper? Well, go outside and get it and call me back." Brenda hung up the phone. They all waited for it to ring again.

"What's taking her so long?" Dylan asked. The phone rang and they all jumped. Brenda answered. Her family sat quietly while she talked to Sarah.

"Okay, thanks, sis, see you soon." Brenda hung up.

"Sarah can't believe it's on the front page. She said she doesn't know anything more than what the paper says. Plus, she's not allowed to talk about it anyway."

"Mom, are you going to let Sarah and Robert come over sometime? It's been a long time since they got married. I miss having Sarah around more." Dylan stood up and put his dishes in the sink.

"Dylan, I told you to stop talking about it," Elizabeth said. "Don't you have to get to school?"

"Yes, but I have time to get ready."

"Did you hear Dylan might ask Heather to the dance that the accounting group is sponsoring?" Brenda asked Elizabeth.

"I did not. Well, that is interesting."

"Come on, you two. I'm right here." Dylan said. "It's true that I might ask her. I think Heather's neat."

"Won't it be a distraction from school?" Elizabeth asked.

"Mom, Heather is lovely. You're so tough on everybody." Brenda shook her head.

"I didn't say anything bad about Heather. I just said she might be a distraction."

"Mom, I'm not twelve anymore. It would be nice to have female companionship. I can't work and study all the time."

Brenda walked over to her mom and gave her a hug. "You are a toughie, Mom. Enjoy that Dylan might go to the dance with Heather. Think about cutting Sarah and Robert some slack. We're all growing up. You need to accept that. Everyone thinks you're being too stubborn."

"Yeah, Mom, Brenda's right," Dylan said.

"There's nothing wrong with being stubborn," said Elizabeth.

"By the way, I keep forgetting to ask. What's the real reason you're mad that Sarah eloped with Robert? I don't think it's because she's young," said Brenda.

"Yeah, Mom, what is it?" Dylan asked.

"She eloped. It's a scandal. Why are you two questioning me?"

"Because it's odd you've been mad for so long. I think there's more to it," Brenda said.

Chapter 25

During her break, Laura walked to the church. It was a gorgeous building, set amongst the trees with a large parking lot behind it. A large white-washed statue of the Virgin Mary stood on the front lawn, surrounded by beautiful purple, blue, and yellow spring flowers. Laura took a deep breath. Ever since the accident at the pharmacy, she'd been upset. She felt so bad for the Miller family.

She went through the side entrance where she ran into Mabel, the church secretary, walking down the hall. "Hi there, Laura. Good to see you. How are you?"

"Good, Mabel. How about you? How are your kids?"

"The kids are doing great. School break can't get here fast enough for them," Mabel said.

"I remember those days. We used to head to the beach as much as we could."

"Father Oliver is back in his office. Feel free to go back. He's expecting you."

"Thanks, Mabel."

Father Oliver was sitting at his typewriter with his back towards the door. He turned and smiled, then stood to shake her hand.

"Laura, come on in. Have a seat. You can close the door behind you if you want." Laura closed it and sat down.

"Oh, Father." She burst into tears. "I'm having such a hard time. I can't believe what's happened to Mrs. Miller.

I feel terrible; she's such a wonderful person. An error like that has never happened before. It's awful."

Father Oliver picked up a box of Kleenex and handed it to Laura who took several tissues and wiped her eyes.

"Laura, it wasn't your fault. I know you feel terrible about it all and it puts a black cloud over life right now. We need to pray for Mrs. Miller. I saw her yesterday and it sounds like she'll be fine eventually. Unfortunately, mistakes happen and we must live with the consequences. You know that neither you nor Henry made the error and you just need to wait until the investigation is complete."

"I know, but they told me I would most likely have to fire the employee who made the error and tell them that they were responsible for this. I can't bear to do that." Laura put her face in her hands and cried.

"Do you know who made the mistake?"

"Henry and I know who it is, but we're waiting until our legal counsel and insurance company advise us on what to do. They're working on all of this behind the scenes."

"Okay then, let them handle it. You can't do anything until they finish. You can't beat yourself up over this. Just keep praying and ask for God's guidance. You and Henry and your pharmacy are an important part of this community. Everyone loves you." Father Oliver put his hands on top of Laura's.

"But what do I do about the Miller family? What do I say or do?"

"Just give them time. Be cordial if you run into them. You could write them a note explaining how you feel, but I would wait until the investigation is complete. Also make sure your lawyer thinks that it's okay to do that."

"I'm just miserable over this. Henry keeps telling me to try to move forward."

"He's right. Try to focus on all the patients you've helped

in this community over the years. You guys have made such a difference in the lives of many." Father Oliver stood up and went over to his bookshelf. Laura watched him scan the titles of the books as his finger ran over them. Finally, his finger stopped on one book and he pulled it off the shelf. He opened it and scanned one of the pages. He sat back down at his desk and handed it to Laura.

"What's this?" Laura asked as she took the book from Father Oliver.

"It's a book on healing," Father Oliver said. "I would read through it. I think it might help you cope. You can borrow it for as long as you like. It's an excellent book. Also, I think this situation will get easier as time goes on and you know more from the investigation. Time does heal. You can't see that now. Also tell Henry he can come by anytime if he needs to talk."

"Henry is handling this a lot better than I am, but I will tell him. Thank you, Father Oliver." Laura stood up and shook Father Oliver's hand.

"You come back anytime, Laura."

Chapter 26

Dylan took his tuxedo out of the closet. He was excited about taking Heather to the dance at his college. They were going out to dinner with Teddy and his date Amy beforehand. He had to pick up Heather in an hour. He'd promised his mom and Brenda that he and Heather would come back so they could take photos. Sarah had come down from the pharmacy to see them dressed up before they left for the dance.

"Dylan, where are you?" Sarah called from the stairwell.

"Just a second, sis, I'm almost ready and then I'll come down to the kitchen." Dylan fixed his tie in the mirror. He grabbed his wallet and car keys and headed down the hallway.

"Here I am, ladies."

"Wow. You clean up nice," Brenda said.

"You sure do." Sarah gave Dylan a kiss on the cheek.

"Hey, watch it, you'll mess up my make-up." Dylan grabbed a cookie off the cooling rack and took a bite.

Eugene walked in from the living room. "Dylan, you look very nice in that tux."

"Let me take a photo." Elizabeth grabbed the camera. "Here, you all get together."

"Mom, I thought we were doing that later." Dylan took another bite from his cookie.

"We'll do it later too but put that cookie down. Come on, let me get a good shot."

"Come on, guys. Line up for your mom." Eugene tried to move them together.

The family took lots of photos. "Enough photos already. I have to go pick up Heather. I'll be back," Dylan said. He opened up the refrigerator and took out the corsage.

"Let me see." Sarah moved in close next to Dylan.

"Wow, Dylan, that is gorgeous. You got great taste, brother. Heather will love it."

"I've never seen him so excited about someone before," Elizabeth said as Dylan headed off.

"Well, Heather is thrilled about going to the dance with him. By the way, Brenda, when are you heading out to England?" Sarah grabbed a cookie from the spatula as Elizabeth lifted it off the cooling rack.

"It's just two weeks away. I can't wait. Harry's been sending me about a letter a day now."

"It's so exciting you going to England and everything. I've always wanted to travel abroad," Sarah said.

"Someday you will. Come on, Mom, we'll help you clean up later. Come over and play scrabble with us," Brenda said.

"Okay, I'm coming," Elizabeth said.

A little later, Dylan arrived back with Heather.

"Oh Heather. You look terrific. Wow, that corsage matches your pink dress perfectly." Sarah stared at Heather.

"You look beautiful," Elizabeth said. The doorbell rang.

"I bet it's Teddy and Amber," Dylan said.

Elizabeth opened the door. "Teddy, wow, you and Miss Amber, you look gorgeous. I love that lavender color on you, Amber."

"Thanks, Mrs. Jones," Amber replied. Teddy's parents came in too.

"Do you mind if we crash the photo session?" Dr. Smith asked.

"Not at all. How are you both?" Elizabeth kissed each of them on the cheek.

"We're terrific. How about you?" Mrs. Smith asked.

"We're fine," Elizabeth said.

"Wow, look at them. I bet you're proud." Mrs. Smith put her hand on Elizabeth's arm.

"I sure am," Elizabeth said.

"How are you, my dear? How's married life treating you?" Mrs. Smith asked Sarah. Dylan hoped his mom wouldn't say anything negative about Sarah's marriage because he wanted the evening to be perfect. He watched Sarah glance at their mother with a worried look on her face before she said, "It's great. We're living down near the river. We love it."

"I'll go get a plate of cookies for everyone." Elizabeth disappeared into the kitchen.

Chapter 27

renda nervously fidgeted in her seat. She'd dressed comfortably for the plane trip. This was her first time flying overseas. It was three hours since they had taken off from JFK airport in New York. She couldn't believe she was on her way to see Harry. They were flying into London then would take a train to Huntingdon. Brenda could hear Harry's father Gabe snoring. The lights were dimmed and most of the passengers had their reading lights off because they were trying to sleep. Brenda couldn't sleep, no matter how hard she tried. She was too excited about seeing Harry.

Brenda had enjoyed talking with Harry's parents and Eva Marie's parents on the bus trip from Connecticut to JFK. She'd learned a lot about their family history. They were a close group and they all wanted Harry to marry and settle down. Harry's mom, Maria, wanted grandbabies. Brenda didn't mind them talking like this; she was head over heels in love with Harry. She fell more in love with him with each letter he sent. He was such a caring and thoughtful man who loved his family dearly. Harry's family loved having Brenda with them on the trip. Harry's parents had even gone so far as to tell the stewardess that Brenda was their future daughter-in-law. Brenda beamed when she heard it.

Brenda closed her eyes and dozed on and off for a while. Once when she woke up she saw Giovanna eyeing her. Brenda yawned and touched the back of her neck. She noticed the lights weren't dimmed anymore.

"My dear, we're almost there. They're going to serve a light breakfast. Would you like something when they come by? I can grab it for you." Giovanna put her tray table down.

"I would love something." Brenda yawned again.

"You've been sleeping for quite some time. But that's a good thing," Giovanna replied. Giovanna took the food from the stewardess when she came by and they began eating breakfast.

"Wow, does that taste good," Brenda said.

"It sure does, they have excellent coffee on this airline," Giovanna replied. An announcement came on that advised them that they were about to land. Brenda's heart started to beat faster. She wasn't used to flying so she wondered how the landing would be. Giovanna must have sensed her anxiety because she grabbed Brenda's hand and held it while they made the descent. Brenda thought of her family back in Connecticut. Brenda was the one that had always had the wild side that wanted to see things outside of New England. The wheels of the plane hit the runway hard. Brenda was startled.

"That was a pretty smooth landing." Giovanna let go of Brenda's hand. The plane taxied slowly to the gate. They gathered their belongings and headed off, going through customs and immigration and then baggage claim. As they left the luggage area, Brenda heard Harry's mom yell "Harry" and saw her embrace someone. Brenda had thought they were meeting Harry in Huntingdon so she was confused but then she spotted Harry in his uniform with his family surrounding him. Harry eyed Brenda with a smile from ear to ear. *Boy, does he look handsome,* she thought. Harry walked through his family and up to her. Brenda's heart raced. He put his arms around her and said, "Hi there, beautiful."

Brenda wrapped her arms around him and didn't want to let go.

Chapter 28

Sarah came into the pharmacy in a pretty pink dress which looked stunning against her dark brown hair.

"Wow, don't we look pretty today," Hazel called from behind the front register. She was talking to Gus who was getting his paper.

"You sure do look nice, Miss Sarah. I heard you and Robert are competing at the Laurelville Fair this weekend in the dance competition." Gus smiled.

"We sure are, Gus. Are you going to come watch?" Sarah asked.

"Well, of course I am, I have to see the home team win," Gus replied.

"Yeah, things sure get crazy in this town when the fair is going on." Hazel said.

"You go, Hazel, don't you?" Sarah asked.

"Well, of course I do. Got to have my orange julip and fried dough. Plus, I love the arts and crafts tents. My good friend Betsy sells her jewelry up there," Hazel said.

"I enjoy seeing all the animals and the country music. Take care, gals, got to get my coffee." Gus walked out the front door. Sarah headed to the back of the store to put her things away and get her smock on.

"Well, hi there, Sarah." Laura was counting pills out for a prescription. Sarah waved to Mrs. Tesh who stood outside the pharmacy area waiting for her medicines.

"Hi, Laura. Thanks for letting me go to that doctor's appointment this morning."

"No problem. Hey, can you help me back here today? I already asked Hazel if she would be okay up front without you."

"I'd love to help back here."

"There's a pile of prescription over there. Could you start pulling the medicines and put them next to the prescriptions?" Laura finished Mrs. Tesh's prescription.

When Laura was done with Mrs. Tesh, she came back and stood next to Sarah. She quietly said, "We had to let Jason go. The investigation determined he had made the error that hurt Mrs. Miller. Our insurance company advised us to let him go."

"Oh no," Sarah said. "He's such a nice man and he has a large family."

"I know, dear. Trust me. This has been extremely hard on everyone. We've lost a lot of sleep over it but it's what we have to do to protect the pharmacy. We'll be looking for someone to replace him but for now Henry and I will be working more to help cover the store." Laura went over to answer the phone. Sarah felt terrible for Jason. She'd known him for several years. Maybe Hazel could explain more of what happened to her later when she had a chance to go up front.

Sarah and Laura worked hard all morning in the pharmacy. Everyone in town seemed to be bringing in prescriptions. At about one o'clock Henry came into the store.

"Hi, honey."

Henry walked over to Laura and gave her a quick kiss on the lips. Sarah admired how well the two of them got along, even working together. She and Robert got along really well, but she didn't know if they could work together.

"Sarah, thanks for helping Laura. You want to take a lunch break now? Then when you come back you want to help Heather in the soda fountain." Henry put on his smock and got right to work.

"Sure thing. I was going to make sandwiches to take to my mom's." Sarah took off her smock and went over to the soda fountain. Heather was waiting on a young couple who had come in for milkshakes and grilled cheese. Sarah grabbed the frying pan.

Heather came over to her. "Just what do you think you're doing in my space, missy?"

"Don't worry, I'll make the sandwiches that you and I need while you make the shakes." Sarah buttered the bread and got the cheese out of the fridge.

"Thanks. I need two BLTs."

Sarah finished making the sandwiches Heather needed. "Here you go. See you in about an hour."

Sarah loved walking at lunchtime. It gave her a chance to relax and gather her thoughts. She and Robert were so excited about the dance competition coming up at the fair. She was going to ask her mom if she would come and watch, but she figured her mom would say no. It was still worth a try.

"Hey, Mom, where are you?" Sarah called as she took the sandwiches out of the bag.

"Here I am. I was just doing some laundry." Elizabeth came into the kitchen and gave Sarah a hug. "You look mighty pretty today."

"Thanks."

"I was looking forward to this. What do you want to drink?" Elizabeth took two glasses from the cupboard.

"I'll take a Fresca."

"How's the pharmacy today?" Elizabeth took a sip of her Fresca.

"Busy, seems like everyone's getting their medicines filled. Also, guess what? They fired Jason. Turns out it was him that made the error. Henry and Laura's insurance company recommended that they fire him. I think there's more to the story, but I haven't had time to figure out what it is."

"Well, that is a shame. I really like Jason and his family. At least they don't live right in town. That will make it easier." Elizabeth took a bite of her sandwich.

"You heard from Brenda?" Sarah asked.

"Not a word. She's in good hands. I think we'll just hear something if anything goes wrong. She did promise to send postcards."

"You going to the fair?" Sarah asked.

"Yes, I promised to help in the church's booth selling food and cold drinks. How about you?"

"We're competing Saturday night in the tango and apache competition. I hope you and Dad might come watch." Sarah looked down at her sandwich.

"Well, maybe we will. Stop by the church booth if you can. Thanks for bringing the sandwiches over. I got some fresh peaches when I went over to the orchards. I cut some up this morning. They're in the fridge if you want some."

"I would love some. You know they're my favorite." Sarah got up and gave her mom a kiss on the top of her head. She got out the bowl of peaches. They smelled so good.

"Oh, these look so good." Sarah took a bite of a peach. "Wow, they are tasty."

"How is it living above the package store?" Elizabeth asked.

"We love it. We have a great view of the river from our bedroom window."

"Doesn't it get loud?"

"No, not at all. They close at eight o'clock and they don't open until ten so it's not bad at all. You need to come by sometime and see our place. It's really cute." Sarah took another bite of a peach as she watched her mother's face.

"Sarah, let's not wreck our time by discussing that right now." Elizabeth grabbed the spoon and put some peaches on her plate.

"Come on, Mom. You need to get over this at some point."

"Why? Robert's parents and whole family knew you were eloping. You didn't bother to tell us anything. Don't you think you were cruel? You made us look like fools."

"Mom, how many times do I have to apologize?"

"I am not asking you to apologize. You just need to accept the fact that I'm still angry."

"Mom, you are so stubborn," Sarah said. She stormed out of the house and slammed the door. She was furious. Her mother had called her cruel for eloping. Sarah cried as she walked down the street towards the pharmacy. She was so confused. She missed hanging out at her mother's house with Robert. Why couldn't things go back to the way they used to be?

Chapter 29

The train was almost at Huntingdon. Brenda sat next to Harry the whole way. She held his hand. She was delighted to be with him. She loved the way he smelled. Brenda felt exhausted from the flight, but the touch of Harry excited her so much that she didn't doze on the train. Harry's parents had their eyes closed. Soon a voice came over the intercom. "Arriving at Huntingdon station, make sure to take all of your belongings."

Harry's parents woke up, startled. Harry laughed.

"You guys were out cold."

"We're old son, we don't have your stamina," Harry's dad said. Outside the station, they found a taxi and were soon traveling towards the house where Brenda would be staying. Harry's dad had gone with his aunt and uncle in a different taxi to their hotel. Brenda was amazed at how they were driving on the wrong side of the road and that the steering wheel was on the opposite side of the car.

"What are we doing again today, Harry? I'm so tired," Harry's mom said.

"We're going to get Brenda all settled in her place. Then we'll take you down to the hotel. Then we can all have a late lunch. How does that sound?"

"Sounds great to me. I'm just so happy to be with you, Harry. I missed you terribly."

"I know, Mom. I miss you all too." Harry smiled at Brenda. The taxi went through the gates of the base. Brenda was impressed at how clean and landscaped it was. Tall trees lined the streets. The taxi stopped in front of a large brick two-story house with white trim.

"Wow, what a gorgeous place," Brenda said when she saw it. Harry rang the doorbell. An attractive blond woman in her fifties came to the door. "Welcome, welcome, you must be Brenda. Harry's told me a lot about you."

Mrs. Singer grabbed Brenda's hand and shook it and then gave her a hug. Then she moved on and gave Maria a hug and said, "You must be Harry's mom, welcome to England. Come on in, let's get Brenda settled."

The house smelled of orange tea and spices. The foyer was gorgeous, with beautiful hardwood floors.

"Just leave your luggage there. Have a seat in the living room. I'll go get you all some tea and scones with cream." Mrs. Singer closed the front door. Brenda walked into the living room. It had a gorgeous fireplace and a large black leather couch with matching loveseat. There was a big orange tabby cat on the loveseat. Brenda walked over and sat down and petted it.

"This place is wonderful. Do we have time for tea or do we need to worry about meeting up with the others?" Brenda asked.

"We'll be fine, dear. They know it will take some time. Trust me, I doubt they mind resting some. It was a long trip."

Harry's mom sat on the couch. Harry sat down next to Brenda on the loveseat. The cat was now on her lap.

"I see you met Pumpkin. She loves people." Mrs. Singer walked into the room and put down the tray. Mrs. Singer sat down next to Harry's mom. She picked up the teapot and poured tea into the mugs. She handed a mug to each of them.

"Thanks so much," Maria said as she took a mug of tea.

"Help yourself to cream and sugar if you like." Mrs. Singer put a scone on each small plate and handed the plates out to everyone.

"This looks great." Brenda took her plate. "What's the best way to eat it?"

"Put on some cream and strawberry jam." Harry took a knife and loaded his with cream and jam. He bit into it. "They're still warm. Mmmm. Delicious."

Brenda followed Harry's lead, then took a bite. "This is so good. Thanks so much, Mrs. Singer. I've never had this before."

"You're welcome dear. I figured you all would be hungry." Mrs. Singer took a sip of her tea. "After we're done, I'll show you your room and give you a key. You're a quick taxi ride to where Harry's family is staying."

"Where are you from originally, Mrs. Singer?" Brenda asked.

"I'm from North Carolina, the Tar Heel State. My husband is from North Carolina as well. We miss it a lot, but we've traveled all over the world. We've been here a couple of years. My husband is a lieutenant colonel. He does logistics so he travels quite a bit. I enjoy having company while he's gone and I love having others from the states stay with me."

"Well, we really appreciate you letting Brenda stay here," Harry's mom said.

When they were finished eating and drinking their tea, Mrs. Singer stood up. "Come on, Brenda, let's go see your room."

There was a double bed in the room with a beautiful quilt covered with red roses. There was a dresser, a red chair with big cushions, and a small table with a lamp next to the bed.

"Feel free to unpack and put your clothes in the dresser and closet. The bathroom is right down the hall. I'll let you get settled. I'm going to head back downstairs and visit with Harry and his mom. I am glad you're here, Brenda."

"Me too," Brenda said. She was so excited to be in England.

Chapter 30

Heather looked stunning.

"Hi Dylan, I'm all ready to go." She gave him a brief kiss on the lips. He felt electrified. She shut the door behind her. "I'm so excited about going to the fair. I'm glad we were both off from classes this afternoon so we could go. Friday is the least busy day."

"Let's just park off of Main Street near the skating pond. Then we can take the bus over to the fair entrance. Does that sound okay to you?"

"That's perfect. If you try to get too close we could be in traffic forever."

Dylan parked and they got out and walked toward the school bus that was loading people to head toward the fair gate. Even the school district dismissed everyone early on the Friday of fair weekend so the students and families could go to the fair to either have fun or work at the booths. The fair was a major source of revenue for many of the local community organizations and school groups.

"Mrs. Conroy," Heather said as they got on the bus, "I didn't know you were still driving the buses."

"I sure am. I'd be miserable if I retired. As long as I can keep passing the driving tests, I'll still be here."

"Well, it's wonderful to see you. You always brightened my day when I had to take the bus to school." Heather patted Mrs. Conroy on the shoulder as she walked by. Dylan loved how good Heather was with people. He felt like a little kid – he loved the fair, especially since he was going with Heather. He still got nervous around Heather. She was so beautiful and smart. When they got to the ticket booth Dylan bought two tickets and handed one to Heather.

"Thanks, Dylan. Where should we head first?"

"How about we head down toward the animals, work our way through the barns and then come back up here? I think Sarah and Robert compete at four in the tango competition." Dylan put his arm around Heather and they started walking.

"Sarah loves to dance and she loves the fancy costumes. She showed me the one she's going to wear. It's quite sexy." Heather winked at Dylan. He blushed.

They walked through the animal barns. They stopped and saw Teddy's bantam chickens. There was a First Place Ribbon on the front of the cage. They couldn't find Teddy but they would see him later at the dance competition. They had all planned to meet there at four o'clock. Heather suddenly grabbed Dylan's hand. "Let's go see the momma pig and babies. They're down this way."

Dylan laughed as he let her pull him toward the pig family. There was a large crowd around the cage. Dylan and Heather stood on their tippy toes to see. They moved up front as people moved away. Dylan studied Heather. She smiled and laughed as the babies climbed all over their mother. Dylan was totally falling for Heather.

"Come on, let's go win you a stuffed animal." Dylan motioned for Heather to follow him toward the door.

"Are you a good shot?"

"Well, I used to be but I guess we'll soon find out if I still am." They stopped at a booth to shoot darts. Dylan totally missed the balloons the first time he played, but his second attempt was more successful.

"Which one of the stuffed animals on this shelf would you like?"

"Heather, you choose," Dylan said.

"I'll take the stuffed owl. It will remind me of you, Dylan, cause you're wise like an owl." Dylan laughed.

"Okay, now let's go play the goldfish game where you throw the ping pongs into the little glass bowls with the goldfish. I'm going to win you something." Heather put her arm around Dylan and they walked toward the goldfish game. Heather won on the first try.

"Wow, you put me to shame."

"Which fish would you like?" the woman asked.

"Do we really want to carry a fish around all night?" Dylan asked.

"No, no," I just wanted to show you that I was a good shot. We won't take a fish." Dylan moved in and gave Heather a kiss on the lips.

"Let's go get a funnel cake on the way to the dance competition area." Heather had her stuffed owl underneath her arm.

Chapter 31

Elizabeth wiped the sweat off her brow. It was crowded and hot. Elizabeth was cooking hamburgers and hot dogs and she loved it. Cooking was one of Elizabeth's favorite things to do and she loved being around her friends from church.

"We need another cheeseburger, Elizabeth," George called from the cash register area.

"You got it, George." Elizabeth put a piece of cheese on a burger and waited while it melted. She loved the hustle and bustle of the fair. Ever since she'd moved to Connecticut she'd been coming to the fair. Elizabeth pulled the burger off of the grill and put it on an open bun which was sitting on a paper plate next to the grill.

"Thank you, Miss Elizabeth." George took the plate. Elizabeth had volunteered to be there when her friends Judy and her husband George were working. Judy was pouring soft drinks. Scott from church was cooking fries and onion rings.

"Two hot dogs, two fries, and two Cokes," George called out. Elizabeth opened two buns and put them on two different plates and then took two hot dogs off of the grill. She brought the plates over to Scott who loaded them with fries. Elizabeth then brought them over to George. He handed them to the customers along with the Cokes that Judy poured.

"It's going to get crowded soon," Judy said to Elizabeth.

"I know. This is so exciting. I love it," Elizabeth said.

"Me too," Judy said.

"Ladies, ladies, get back to work. I need two cheeseburgers, one hot dog, two fries, two Cokes, and a Sprite," George said.

"Hey, we're taking you off of that cash register soon and putting you on the grill." Judy began to pour the drinks.

"Hey, Mom, hey." Elizabeth looked up and saw Dylan and Heather. She smiled. She was glad Dylan was dating Heather. Heather was taking classes with the hopes of going to pharmacy school one day and she made Dylan happy.

"Well, hi, you two. You been having fun?"

"We sure have. Check out what Dylan won for me." Heather held up the stuffed owl.

"That is adorable," Judy said as she put the drinks down in front of George.

"Can I buy you two anything to eat?" Elizabeth asked.

"No, we've been grazing all afternoon. Sarah dances pretty soon. We're going to head over that way so we can get a good view. We just wanted to say hi," Dylan said.

"Well, thanks for coming by and have fun." Elizabeth pulled the burgers and hot dogs off the grill. Father Clark and his wife Rose came into the booth.

"We're here to help." Father Clark put his arm around George.

"Well, you're here in the nick of time. Sarah and Robert are competing soon in the dance competition and Elizabeth wanted to go watch." Judy smiled at Elizabeth. *I'm going to get her back for this,* Elizabeth thought.

"I, I..."

"Well, you go on, Elizabeth. I can take over the grill." Father Clark put on an apron and grabbed a spatula.

"Yeah, Judy, you go with her. I can take over the drinks.

Just come back over when she's done dancing because that's
about when it will get super busy." Rose put on an apron.

"Come on, Elizabeth." Judy took off her apron.

"I'm going to kill you," Elizabeth said to Judy as they
walked into the crowds.

"You need to get over being mad at Robert for eloping
with Sarah. You've been angry for too long. Plus, I love you,
my friend, and I know you love watching Sarah dance." Judy
put her arm around Elizabeth. They walked through the
fair towards the competition area. The crowds were growing in size. It was tough to navigate through all the people.
Elizabeth planned to stand in the back so that Sarah wouldn't
see her there. They walked into the dance competition area
and Elizabeth stopped for a second in the back. There was a
young couple on stage doing a ballroom dance. The woman
had on a gorgeous light Carolina blue gown and the man a
black tuxedo with a Carolina blue tie. Elizabeth loved hearing the ballroom dance music; it relaxed her some.

"I guess we still have a little more time before they start
the tango competition. Glad we got here on time. Why don't
we go closer?" Judy asked.

"I'll stay right here, thank you. In fact, let's climb up
there." Elizabeth pointed to the bleachers.

"Okay, grumpy," Judy said. Elizabeth headed to the front
of the bleachers and started climbing up. Judy followed her
up toward the top. They sat down at the very top. The judges
were announcing who had won the ballroom competition below. The couple that Elizabeth and Judy saw dancing when
they walked in won first place. Elizabeth saw that Heather
and Dylan had come in. They moved toward the front of
those who were standing near the bleachers. Elizabeth was
relieved that they didn't notice her.

"Alright, ladies and gentlemen, now we move to the

tango. We have five couples that are finalists. First up are Sarah and Robert."

Sarah and Robert came out on the stage. Sarah was in a gorgeous V-neck black dress, bright red lipstick and a red bow in her hair. She had on black high heels.

"Wow, she looks great, Elizabeth," Judy said.

"She sure does. And look at Robert. He looks great in his black tux and I love his red bow tie. They look sharp together." Elizabeth watched as Sarah and Robert waited for the music to start. As the music began, Sarah and Robert started moving rhythmically together across the stage. Judy and Elizabeth and the rest of the audience were mesmerized. Elizabeth loved hearing the crowd clap as Sarah and Robert danced. When they finished the dance, everyone stood, clapped, and cheered. So did Elizabeth. Robert and Sarah took a bow and then gracefully exited the stage. Elizabeth and Judy stayed to watch the next four couples. Elizabeth didn't think that any were as good as Sarah and Robert. Neither did Judy. Then all five couples were called on the stage. The announcer took out a card. "That was a marvelous competition. Great job everyone. Our winners are... Sarah and Robert."

Elizabeth watched Sarah and Robert take their trophy. The crowd roared. Sarah looked extremely happy to Elizabeth. Sarah and Robert then moved backstage with the other dancers.

"Elizabeth, you must be proud. How terrific. Now we better get back to help at the booth." Judy stood.

"No, no. Wait a minute. Let's wait until Dylan and Heather leave. I don't want them to see me." Elizabeth stayed seated. Judy sat back down and shook her head. Finally, when Dylan and Heather left the dance area, Elizabeth and Judy headed back to the church booth.

"Hey, Elizabeth, Sarah looked fantastic," Judy said.

"She sure did." Elizabeth had noticed that Sarah looked like she had a baby bump. She wondered if her daughter was pregnant.

"You okay? You look a little pale."

"I'm fine. Just a little overheated I think." Elizabeth said. Elizabeth felt confused. What if Sarah was pregnant? She'd be a grandmother. But what about Robert? She was still angry he'd convinced Sarah to elope. But she might be a grandmother. She would have a little one to spoil and teach things. How grand life would be.

Chapter 32

Brenda loved living at Mrs. Singer's house. She and Mrs. Singer had tea and scones on the afternoons that Brenda wasn't out sightseeing. Sometimes she and Harry's family went sightseeing in the area's towns and some days they just all hung out locally. Harry had to work most days. He worked on the line that fixed and maintained the planes' radars. He had received a lot of training in engineering since he joined the air force. The pilots based at Alconbury flew many different types of missions.

Brenda especially loved the evenings on the base. She and Harry would often eat at the mess hall together. Then they would go on walks together. They walked all over the base. They would hold hands and just talk. Harry made her feel at peace. She was so happy to be able to see him every day.

Sometimes they would go into Huntingdon and walk along the Alconbury Brook. Brenda especially enjoyed walking over the Nun's Bridge which was supposedly haunted by the ghost of a nun. Hinchingbrooke House stood near the bridge. It had been a convent in the past. Legend had it that the nun who haunted the bridge had had a lover who was a monk and that when their affair was discovered, both were killed. Brenda thought the story was tragic.

Brenda was waiting for Harry on Mrs. Singer's front lawn. They were going to take a cab into town to go to a nice restaurant. Harry's family was eating at their hotel tonight so it would just be the two of them. Brenda was wearing a new dark blue dress with a white collar and buttons that she'd bought in Huntingdon. She and Harry's family had spent the day in Huntingdon. Brenda loved all the British styles. They had gorgeous dresses and jewelry. Harry's mom and his aunt also each bought a dress. They had eaten lunch at a pub. Brenda had had fish and chips. Brenda really enjoyed Harry's family. His family were really close, just like her own family.

Brenda spotted Harry walking up the road. She thought he looked handsome in his uniform. It took her breath away. She was so in love with him. Brenda stood up and walked down the front sidewalk.

"Well, hi there, beautiful. Don't you look gorgeous?" Harry walked up to Brenda and took her in his arms and kissed her passionately.

Brenda loved it but pushed away. "Harry, what if Mrs. Singer's watching?"

"Well, if she is watching, I bet she's wishing she could kiss her husband like that right now," Harry said.

"Yeah, but she's married."

"Well, maybe one day we'll be married too," Harry said. "Now come on, we need to walk down to the base hotel and get a cab."

Harry grabbed Brenda's hand and they walked down the road towards the mess hall. As they passed by the different homes on the base, they waved at the families who were outside in their yards. People on the base were extremely supportive of one another. This helped when the men got deployed. When they arrived at the base hotel, Harry went up to a man working out front and asked for a taxi. One of them grabbed a phone and called a taxi for Harry. A few minutes later, a taxi pulled up and they got in.

"Where to?" the driver asked.

"The George Hotel. I'm taking my girl out for a nice dinner." Harry grabbed Brenda's hand.

"Good choice. We'll be there shortly." The driver pulled out into the street and headed toward the gate to get them off of base and into town. Harry held onto Brenda's hand all the way into town. She loved being next to him. It was nice to have a dinner date with just him. She enjoyed his family but she cherished the time she got alone with Harry. She knew that this was why she was staying with Mrs. Singer rather than at the hotel. Mrs. Singer was like a chaperone to the girls that stayed with her. Harry's family had to make sure that they didn't have too much alone time together.

The taxi pulled in front of the hotel. It was in a beautiful old white stone house with pretty flowers planted in all of the windows. There were candles in the windows too. Brenda followed Harry inside.

"I have a reservation. Harry Rigoni. Table for two," Harry told the host. The man grabbed two menus and led them to a quiet table in the back.

"Perfect," Harry said. Brenda sat across from him. Small candles glistened in the middle of the table. A small red vase held two red roses.

"Wow. Harry, this is wonderful. How romantic." Brenda grabbed his hand from across the table.

"Anything for my girl. I'm so glad to get some time just with you. My family loves you so much, but I can't get enough of you for myself." Harry squeezed Brenda's hand. A waiter came up to their table.

"Welcome. What can I get you to drink?"

"Brenda, are you in the mood for red or white wine or beer?" Harry asked.

"How about some white wine?"

"We'll take a bottle of house white. Whatever you think is best." Harry opened his menu.

"What are you going to get?" Brenda scanned the menu.

"I'm in the mood for a big steak. Steak and potatoes. How about you?" Harry closed his menu.

"I was thinking of lamb. The lamb chops with mint and mashed potatoes look yummy."

"I'm looking forward to tomorrow and having a day off. It's been busy at work this week. They're doing a lot of flights lately." Harry took a sip of water.

"I'm glad too. Let's hope the weather holds out so we can go on a picnic like we planned," Brenda said. The waiter came back with the bottle of white wine.

"Are you ready to order?"

"Yes, we are."

After they ordered, Harry raised his glass and said, "Let's have a toast."

"To the love of my life. You are the light of my life." Harry clinked his glass against Brenda's glass. Brenda welled up with tears.

Harry reached into his inside coat pocket and pulled out a small blue box. He opened the box. "Brenda, will you make me the happiest man on earth and marry me?"

Brenda gasped. The box held a gorgeous one carat diamond ring. "Oh, my gosh. Yes, yes, I'd love to marry you Harry."

Chapter 33

Elizabeth yawned as she scoped coffee into the percolator. She'd woken up exhausted. Working at the church's fair booth the day before had worn her out. Eugene was in the shower. She'd decided not to mention Sarah's bump to Eugene. She had to think more about her suspicion. Even though she was angry at Sarah for marrying Robert so young, she would be thrilled if Sarah was pregnant. That would mean that she would be a grandmother.

Dylan walked into the kitchen. He kissed Elizabeth on the cheek. "Morning, Mom."

"Where are you off to so early?"

"Teddy and I are heading down to New Haven. We're helping out at a fundraiser for Special Olympics, then we're coming back and going to the fair." Dylan opened the cupboard and took out a box of Cheerios.

"Do you want me to make you some eggs?"

"No thanks. I ate too much last night at the fair." Dylan patted his stomach. Elizabeth laughed.

"Was that you at the dance competition?"

"What?" Elizabeth took cream out of the refrigerator.

"Don't try to snow me, Mom. I saw you up top with Judy watching the show." Dylan poured cereal into his bowl. Elizabeth turned red. "Don't worry, Mom. I won't rat you out to Sarah. I think it's nice that you went. Didn't she look gorgeous and happy?"

"She sure did. Did you have a nice time with Heather?"

"I did. She's pretty awesome. She has to work all day today. Sarah does too. The soda fountain does a killer business on fair weekend." Dylan got the milk out of the refrigerator and poured some into his cereal bowl. When the coffee was ready Elizabeth poured herself a cup and sat down at the table with Dylan.

"What are you up to today, Mom?" Dylan asked.

"I'm heading to Milltown to do some shopping. I'm going to stop in and see Aunt Abbey." Elizabeth took a sip of coffee.

"You're going to see Abbey? I didn't know that." Eugene walked into the kitchen and poured himself a cup of coffee.

"Yes. I just decided to. I feel like shopping today and so I figured I'd go visit Abbey and see if she wants to play some cards."

"Cards? It's Saturday. They'll be busy at the bakery," Eugene said.

"Why are you questioning me so much?" Elizabeth asked.

"What's got into you? I just think it's odd you say you're going to play cards on a Saturday at a busy bakery."

"Well, maybe we won't play cards but I figure I might as well say hello since I'll be over her way anyway." Elizabeth stood up and put her coffee cup in the sink. She grabbed her purse and keys.

"Aren't you going to make bacon and eggs?" Eugene asked.

"Not this morning. You're on your own if you want them. See you two this afternoon."

"Elizabeth. What on earth are you doing here?" Abbey was wiping down the bakery cases.

"Have to talk to you. Need advice." Elizabeth walked over to Abbey and gave her a hug.

"Well, let's grab some coffee and sit down. My feet need a break. It felt like the whole town was in here for donuts and rolls. Want a donut?"

"I'd love a jelly donut." Elizabeth put her purse on one of the tables and helped Abbey get the coffee and donuts.

"How was the fair?" Abbey asked.

"The crowds were large. Aren't you going this year?"

"No. We decided not to." Abbey put the donuts on the table while Elizabeth put the coffee mugs down. They sat down.

"I hope it stays quiet like this just for a little while." Abbey sipped her coffee.

"Where's Joe?"

"He went to the store to get some supplies. So, what's up?"

"Well. I went and watched Sarah and Robert dance at the fair." Elizabeth took a bite of her donut.

"Oh, I wish I could have seen them. Oh no, did they lose? Was she upset?" Abbey took a sip of coffee.

"Actually, they won."

"So, what's the problem then?"

"She had a bump."

"A bump? A bump, where?" Abbey asked.

Elizabeth put her hands on her stomach. "Here."

"Oh my God. You think she's pregnant?" Abbey slapped Elizabeth on the back.

"Yes. Yes," Elizabeth said.

"You'd be a grandmother. Oh, my goodness," Abbey said.

"But what do I do? What do I say? How do I find out for sure?"

"You ask her, silly."

Chapter 34

Robert sat on the stool at the pharmacy while Sarah and Heather worked the soda fountain crowd. He'd already had a butterscotch sundae, a Coke, and a root beer float. He was super full. If Sarah didn't get off work soon, he felt like he would fall into a sugar stupor. Robert had come over an hour ago to pick her up. They were so busy because of the fair that she'd already worked over an hour later than she was supposed to. Even though the seats at the soda fountain were full, people kept coming in and ordering milkshakes, floats, and sundaes to go.

Sarah handed a man his vanilla shake and root beer float. He took money out of his wallet and handed it to Sarah. "Keep the change. You two are the hardest working soda jerks I've ever seen."

Sarah smiled. She threw the change into the tip jar by the cash register. Sarah thought it was funny when people referred to her and Heather as soda jerks. She actually liked being called that.

"I'll never get used to being called a soda jerk. It's so odd," Heather said.

"I told you it's because of the jerking movement we make when we add the soda water to different ice cream drinks. He complimented us." Sarah scooped ice cream into a bowl.

"Well, you two are the cutest soda jerks I've ever seen." Dylan walked over to them.

"Dylan." Heather gave him a light kiss. "You're here early."

"Wanted to see my girl. Teddy and I got back early. Hey there, Robert." Dylan patted Robert on the back.

"Hi, Dylan. Good to see you."

"You guys were awesome last night." Dylan sat down next to Robert.

"Thanks, Dylan. It was all your sister." Robert winked at Sarah who smiled.

"Did you know Mom was there watching?"

"She was?" Robert asked.

"Yes, she was way up top with Judy. They took a break from working the church booth to see you dance. Now don't tell her I told you, but I think that's a huge step for Mom. Hey, can I just get a Coke?"

"I'll get it," Heather told Sarah.

"Wow, that's amazing. Maybe she's softening up." Sarah looked perplexed.

"She's a stubborn woman," Robert said. "That's part of what I've always liked about her, she digs her heels in. I just didn't think she'd dig them in this much."

Sarah started wiping down the counters. Robert hoped that meant they could leave soon. Laura walked over from the pharmacy area. She patted Robert on the back. "Okay, drugstore cowboy, looks like you can finally take your sweet wife out of here. I never thought the crowds would die down."

"Thanks, Laura. Let me just clean up a little." Sarah took the dirty glasses to the sink.

"You go on ahead. I'll help Heather clean up. The pharmacy area is quiet. Gives me a chance to catch up with Heather and Dylan." Laura put on an apron as she walked behind the soda fountain.

"Thanks, Laura," Sarah said.

"Also, your mom just called, she asked if you could stop

by after work. I told her Robert was here so she said you both should stop by." Laura rinsed the dishes in the sink.

"Oh no, wonder what that means," Dylan said.

"She really said for both of us to stop by?" Sarah asked.

"Yes," Laura said. Robert suddenly felt sick to his stomach.

"I'll be right back." Sarah went in the back to grab her things and clock out.

Robert stood up. "What you two doing tonight?"

"Just going over to Heather's to hang out and watch a movie," Dylan said.

"Sounds like you'll have more fun than we're going to have," Robert said. Sarah grabbed his arm.

"See you all later." Sarah waved.

"Guess we better go see what she wants," Sarah said as she got into the car.

"This is going to be awkward."

Eugene and Elizabeth were watching television in the living room. Robert felt nervous. He hadn't spoken to Elizabeth in months. They had been close before he'd eloped with Sarah. He missed her friendship. Eugene was pleasant to him whenever they saw each other. It was Elizabeth he was afraid of.

"Hi. We're in here. Thanks for coming," Elizabeth called. Robert and Sarah walked into the living room. Eugene stood up and shook Robert's hand. He gave Sarah a hug. Elizabeth remained seated in her rocking chair. "Have a seat. Can I get you anything to drink?"

"No thanks, Mom. We just left the pharmacy." Sarah sat down on the couch. Robert sat next to her and held her hand.

He could tell Sarah was just as nervous as he was because her pulse was so fast.

"What's up, Mom?" Sarah asked.

"Well, I went to your dance competition last night and I have to say you two were absolutely marvelous."

"Thanks for coming to watch us." Sarah squeezed Robert's hand harder.

"I just had a quick question," Elizabeth said.

"What's that?" Sarah asked.

"Are you pregnant?"

"What?" Eugene looked confused.

"Are you pregnant?" Elizabeth asked again.

"Yes. I am."

Chapter 35

Brenda woke up and looked at her finger. What a gorgeous ring. She was engaged. She couldn't believe it. She felt like she was in heaven. She couldn't wait to show Mrs. Singer. She jumped up and put on her robe and slippers and headed down the stairs. Mrs. Singer was in the kitchen reading the newspaper and drinking tea. She looked up when she heard Brenda coming towards her. "Well, good morning, Brenda. Want some tea? Did you have fun last night?"

"Look, look, check this out." Brenda put her left hand in front of Mrs. Singer.

"Oh, my goodness. You're engaged. How wonderful. Congratulations." Mrs. Singer stood up and gave Brenda a hug.

"I couldn't believe it. I wasn't expecting it. He proposed right in the restaurant at the George Hotel." Brenda squealed with delight. "I so wish I could tell my sister, Sarah. She would love it. She just got married herself less than a year ago."

"Do you want to call her?"

"No, no. Even though I'd love to tell my whole family, I'd rather to see their faces when I show them the ring." Mrs. Singer poured Brenda a cup of tea and handed it to her.

"Have you seen Harry's family since he proposed?"

"No, Harry and I just spent a wonderful evening alone in

town and then he dropped me off here before going back to the barracks last night. I'll see them today. We're all going to Cambridge." Brenda took a couple of quick sips of tea. "In fact, I better go get ready because I'm supposed to walk down and meet Harry outside the barracks."

Brenda walked down to the barracks. It was a gorgeous sunny day. The skies were bright blue which was rare for this part of England. Harry came up and gave her a huge hug when he spotted her.

"Let's get a cab, beautiful. I am so excited. My family's going to go crazy when we see them."

They found Harry's family in the breakfast room in the hotel. "My dear, show us, show us, we heard he was popping the question last night." Harry's mom grabbed Brenda's left hand.

"Oh, my gosh, look at that ring, absolutely gorgeous - like the woman wearing it." Maria gave Brenda a kiss on the cheek. "We're so glad you'll become a part of our family."

"We sure are." Harry's dad gave Brenda a hug. Brenda was teary-eyed. She was so happy inside.

"What's going on over here?" Harry walked up with a big smile.

"Harry, we're so happy for you. Congratulations. We're thrilled she said yes," Harry's mom said.

"What, did you think she'd say no?" Harry smiled at Brenda.

The family went to the botanical gardens at the university. Brenda read a sign that said the gardens were created by a professor who was Charles Darwin's mentor. The gardens were first opened to the public in 1846. Brenda thought it was amazing to be standing in gardens that had existed for over a hundred years.

They decided they wanted to go on a guided punting tour. Harry and Brenda had their own punt. Each punt had a guide who moved them down the river. The scenery was spectacular. Brenda thought it was very romantic. She held Harry's hand as they were guided through the river. Every now and then she would see her engagement ring glisten in the sunlight. Her heart raced each time.

"Okay, now let's head over to the chapel at the college," Harry's mother said. Harry's mom loved chapels and churches. Brenda didn't mind seeing the historic sites. The scenery was gorgeous and she loved being with Harry and his family. She thought of her own family. She was getting homesick. She couldn't wait to tell them about this wonderful trip and the engagement. Just a few more days and she would have to head back to Connecticut. Even though she would be thrilled to see her family, she dreaded the thought of leaving Harry.

Chapter 36

Sarah couldn't believe that her mother had figured out she was pregnant. If her mother had figured it out then others must suspect it too. She'd wanted to wait a few more weeks before telling everyone, but she decided she better start telling people. She wished Brenda was there to tell but she wouldn't be home for a few more days. Sarah hoped Dylan would stop by the pharmacy today so she could tell him. Her mother had promised not to tell him so that Sarah could. She decided to just call Dylan.

"Hi Dad, can I talk to Dylan?" Sarah asked.

"Hi, sis, what is up?"

"Do you have time to meet up for a coffee or Coke sometime today? I work from twelve to six. I need to talk to you about something."

"Sure, how about I meet you at the bakery at eleven thirty for coffee? I have late classes today," Dylan said.

"Great. See you then." Sarah hung up the phone. Perfect, she thought, because then she could tell people at the pharmacy after she spoke to Dylan. Sarah was excited about being pregnant and she felt relieved that she could finally tell people. She was happy that her mother had taken the news so well and that the feud between her mother and Robert was finally over.

"Hi Dylan," Sarah hugged him as he came up to her. "Thanks for meeting me."

"This better be good, sis. Although I didn't mind coming up here because it gives me an excuse to stop by and see Heather." They walked into the bakery. They sat down with their drinks while their sandwiches were being made.

"So, what's up?" Dylan asked.

"Well, I, I'm pregnant and I wanted to tell you in person," Sarah said.

"Wow, sister, how cool is that! Congratulations. I'm so happy for you guys." He leaned over and gave her a hug.

"I'm due in about six months. We're really excited."

"Does Mom know yet?"

"Yes, she figured it out after watching me dance. Can you believe it? She asked me yesterday if I was." Sarah took a sip of her Pepsi.

"Hey, should you be drinking that?" Dylan asked.

"Yes, it's fine. It's only one." Sarah rolled her eyes. The woman working at the bakery brought over their sandwiches. As the bakery door opened, a bell jingled. Sarah looked up and saw Gary walk through the front door. Sarah waved at Gary as he went up to order a sandwich. Gary gave Sarah a fake smile. He did not look happy to see her. He turned his back to her when he got to the counter to order.

"You and Heather getting pretty serious?" Sarah asked. She wondered why Gary was acting rude.

"We have a good time together. I don't know what you mean about serious." Dylan took a bite of his sandwich.

"I'm just happy for you, brother, that's all," Sarah said. They watched Gary walk out the door with his sandwich.

"What do you think of Gary?" Sarah asked.

"Why?"

"Does he seem strange to you?"

"Well, you know what they say about him?"

"No, I don't know." Sarah took a sip of her Pepsi.

"You know. He doesn't like girls," Dylan quietly said under his breath. Sarah's heart sank.

"I didn't know that." Sarah looked shocked. She wondered if she should tell Dylan that she thought she saw Gary in Elkton. She decided not to mention it to Dylan because Robert had sworn it wasn't Gary.

Dylan and Sarah both finished their sandwiches and then walked over to the pharmacy. When they walked in together, Heather smiled.

"Look who I found in a dark alley," Sarah said as she walked toward the back to put her things away. Dylan stopped at the soda fountain to talk with Heather.

"Hi there, Sarah." Laura looked up from counting out pills for a prescription.

"Hi, Laura." Sarah put her purse in the cubie and grabbed her smock.

"Can you help me back here right now? The soda fountain has been kind of quiet but we have lots of prescriptions to fill. Henry doesn't come in for another hour." Laura pointed to the pile of prescriptions on the counter.

"Sure, I'd love to help." Sarah put on her smock and picked up a prescription.

"I hope you don't mind me asking but was everything okay with your mom Saturday night? She never calls the pharmacy," Laura asked.

"Yes, everything's fine. Thanks for asking. You gave me a perfect lead in for what I need to tell you," Sarah whispered. "I'm pregnant. My mom suspected it."

"Pregnant, how wonderful." Laura put down the prescription she was working on and gave Sarah a hug. *I wonder why everyone hugs a pregnant woman*, Sarah thought.

"But can we keep it between us for right now? I still need to tell Heather."

"Of course, dear. I'm so happy for both of you. How'd your mom take it?"

"She was thrilled. I wish I could tell Brenda but she won't be back from England for a few more days. I thought of calling her but then I decided to wait and tell her in person." Sarah started counting out pills.

"Good idea. She'll be so excited and think of all the stories she'll have from England. I'm so happy to hear about your mom being happy."

"Is today the day you have one of the pharmacist candidates coming in to interview?" Sarah asked.

"Yes. We're interviewing three different pharmacists for Jason's position. I still feel bad that we had to let him go. Did I tell you Mrs. Miller called me?"

"No. What did she say?"

"Well, I was quite shocked that it was her and I immediately started worrying that she'd start yelling or something, but guess what she did?"

"What?" Sarah asked.

"She told me that Henry and I had always been good to her and that her daughter had heard we'd fired Jason because of the error that he'd made. She thanked us for doing that. She won't pursue legal action against us anymore. She'd talked to Father Oliver." Laura put the filled prescription in a bag.

"Wow, that's amazing. Well, you're wonderful people and you do great things for everyone who gets their prescriptions filled here. It's too bad about Jason but I'm sure he'll find a job somewhere else."

"Actually, he already did. He decided to take a job in a hospital pharmacy. He starts next week. The hospital called me for a reference. They knew about the whole situation. You'll get to meet the first pharmacist we're interviewing around two. His name is Richard. He lives over in Robinsville. He sounds like a nice young man." Laura walked over to the pick-up window to ring up the young woman waiting for her prescription.

Just before two o'clock, a handsome young man in his mid-twenties came in. He had sparkling blue eyes and jet-black hair. "Is Laura here?" he asked.

Wow, Sarah thought. "Laura's in the back office. Let me see if she's available. Can I tell her who's asking?"

"My name's Richard; I'm here to interview for the pharmacist job," Richard said. Sarah spotted Heather staring at them from the soda fountain.

"I'm Sarah, welcome, let me see if she's ready for you." Sarah held out her hand. Richard shook it. Sarah walked to the back office and lightly tapped on the door. She knew Laura was trying to eat a quick sandwich.

"Come in," Laura said.

"Richard's here," Sarah closed the door halfway behind her and whispered, "He's quite the looker."

"Is Henry back yet?"

"No."

"Tell him to come on back. I'll start without Henry." Sarah showed Richard into the office and then went back to finish filling prescriptions so Laura could check them. Heather and Hazel rushed over.

"He's a looker. I sure hope they hire him." Heather grabbed Sarah's hands with excitement.

"Girls, girls. Now he may be a looker but let's hope he's smart too," Hazel said.

"I have something I need to tell you both," Sarah said. "I'm pregnant."

"No wonder Dylan was smiling from ear to ear after

he talked to you. Congratulations, that is so wonderful."
Heather hugged Sarah.

"You'll make a terrific mother. Congratulations, Sarah,"
Hazel said.

Chapter 37

renda held Harry's hand as they took the train to London. She dreaded leaving him. She put her head on his shoulder and he put his arm around her. Brenda didn't want to cry.

"I'll see you in two short months when I have a two-week break. We can look around and figure out where we want to have our wedding next year when I'm back." Harry fiddled with Brenda's engagement ring.

"I know, I know, it's just that two months is a long time."

"It'll go fast and I promise I'll write every day." Harry put his head next to hers.

"Make sure to get all of your belongings," a man called over the loudspeaker. Brenda turned and looked up at a Harry. He gave her a long passionate kiss before his parents stood up to start gathering their bags. Brenda didn't want the kiss to stop but Harry stood up to help with all the bags. Brenda wiped tears from her eyes and turned so no one could see. The train came to a stop and they all got off. Harry grabbed a couple of carts and put all of their baggage on it. The family started walking toward the airport terminal. Brenda's stomach ached.

"Well, son, this has been an absolutely wonderful trip." Harry's mom put her arm around him. "And now we have a wedding to look forward to."

"We sure do." Harry's dad put his arm around Brenda. "You couldn't be marrying a better girl."

Brenda blushed. "Well, I feel honored to become part of your family. I can't wait to get home and tell my family. They'll be thrilled."

"Let's hope," Harry's mom said. "Your mom sure didn't react well to Sarah's marriage."

"Well, she says it's because Sarah is so young and that she eloped, but I don't know. Maybe there's some other reason why she was so against the marriage that none of us know," Brenda said. They arrived at the ticket counter and checked in. Harry waited as their bags were tagged and they got their boarding passes. Once Brenda was done checking in, Harry walked over to her and put his arm around her. She wished she could just stay in England with him.

"Which way is our gate?" Harry's mom asked.

"This way," Harry's dad replied. The family walked towards the gate and security.

"Well, Harry, I guess this is it." Harry's dad gave him a hug and walked toward security. Harry's aunt and uncle did the same. His mother became teary-eyed as she hugged him goodbye. "I love you, Harry."

The family all moved toward security to give Brenda and Harry privacy. They embraced and Brenda burst into tears. "I'm going to miss you terribly."

"And I you, but we have to be positive." Harry leaned in to kiss Brenda. She felt his warm tears on her cheek as he did.

Chapter 38

Elizabeth checked on the roast she had in the oven. Today was a big occasion. Brenda was arriving back from England around five o'clock. Elizabeth couldn't wait to see her; she'd worried about her the whole time she was abroad. They'd just received a postcard from her that was hanging on the refrigerator. It sounded like Brenda had had a great time with Harry and his family.

Sarah and Robert and Abbey and Joe were coming over for dinner too. Elizabeth looked forward to her family being all together. Eugene came into the kitchen. "Wow, that roast smells fantastic."

"It sure does, doesn't it? It should be done on time." Elizabeth closed the oven door.

"I'll run up to the store and get a couple bottles of wine. You need anything else?"

"No, I'm good. I just need to peel the potatoes. Abbey's bringing dessert and Sarah told me she made coleslaw."

"Okay then, see you in a little while." Elizabeth had just begun peeling the potatoes when Dylan and Teddy came in.

"Hey, Mom. It sure smells good in here." Dylan threw his book bag down on the kitchen table.

"Yeah Mrs. Jones. It sure does smell awesome," Teddy said.

"What are you two up to?" Elizabeth asked as she peeled the potatoes.

"Well, we just got done studying so we were going to watch the game on television down at Teddy's," Dylan replied.

"That's fine, but just remember to come back up by five," Elizabeth said.

"Will do, Mom." Dylan headed back out the door, leaving his book bag on the table.

"Bye, Mrs. Jones."

"Bye, Teddy." Elizabeth was glad that her children seemed happy. Dylan was really enjoying dating Heather and studying accounting in college. Hopefully Brenda had had a good trip with Harry. And Sarah was pregnant. Elizabeth couldn't wait to be a grandmother. It gave her purpose and something to look forward to. There was a knock at the door.

"Abbey, what are you doing here?" Elizabeth said as she opened the door.

"I figured I'd come early and help you get ready. Joe is coming by later." Abbey was carrying a chocolate cake and some loaves of bread.

"Here, let me help you." Elizabeth grabbed the bread and shut the door.

"Wow, it smells great in here." Abbey put the cake down on the counter.

"You want anything to drink?" Elizabeth asked.

"I'd love a Pepsi. Can I grab one?"

"Of course, of course," Elizabeth replied. "Let me just finish peeling these potatoes."

"You never told me what happened when you confronted Sarah."

"Sarah wants to tell you herself." Elizabeth wiped her brow.

"That means she is pregnant. How exciting."

"Now I didn't tell you, don't get me in trouble." Elizabeth turned on the stove.

"I won't say anything. Does this mean you'll talk to Robert now?" Abbey said.

"Yes, he's coming with Sarah tonight."

"Well, I'm glad. Robert's a good guy. I never understood why you stopped talking to him." Abbey sat down at the kitchen table.

"They shouldn't have eloped. Sarah is so young. But if they're going to have a baby, then I need to be supportive." Elizabeth sat down with Abbey.

"I agree with that. You need to support them and spoil your future grandbaby. We'll have to plan a baby shower."

"That would be great, Abbey. We can ask Heather and Brenda to help us figure out who to invite." Elizabeth clasped her hands with excitement. The water started boiling over on the stove. Elizabeth got up, turned the burner down, and stirred the potatoes.

"What can I do to help you?" Abbey stood up.

"Want to cut the ends off of the green beans for me and put them in the pot? I've already washed them."

"Sure."

"I'll start setting the dining room table while you work on the green beans." Elizabeth took her nicest tablecloth out of the linen drawer. The tablecloth was white and embroidered with blue flowers. She grabbed her china out of the cabinet and set it out on the table. The china was decorated with tiny blue flowers. Elizabeth was so excited that all her family was coming over. She was glad that she and Robert and Sarah could be at peace with one another. *Thank goodness for the future grandbaby,* she thought. The front door suddenly opened and in walked Brenda.

"Oh my gosh, I'm so glad you're home safe." Elizabeth rushed over to Brenda, who dropped her bag and gave her mom a big hug.

"Hi, Aunt Abbey." Brenda turned to greet her aunt.

"You look so pretty, Brenda," Abbey said. "I love your dress."

"I bought several in England. I just love their styles."

"Is that a ring on your finger?" Abbey asked. Elizabeth turned, bewildered. *A ring,* she thought.

"Why, congratulations. How beautiful. I'm so excited for you." Abbey hugged Brenda.

"Mom?" Brenda looked at her mom, not quite sure how she would react.

"I'm so happy for you dear. Harry is a good man. Let me see the ring." Elizabeth stared at the ring and smiled. "Gorgeous." She embraced Brenda. *Brenda is older and more mature than Sarah and ready to get married,* Elizabeth thought. Dylan suddenly walked through the door followed by Eugene who was carrying some bottles of wine.

"Sis, I thought I saw you being dropped off. How the heck are you?" Dylan embraced Brenda.

"I had a great time in England," Brenda said.

"And check out her finger," Elizabeth said. Brenda put her left hand out so everyone could see.

"Wow. Congrats, sis. Harry is a lucky guy." Dylan stared at the diamond.

"Congratulations, Brenda. Soon I'll have both my daughters married off," Eugene said.

Chapter 39

Robert saddled his horse while Gary and Steve took their horses out of the barn. Robert loved animals. He always had. They relaxed him. Steve's family had a large farm in town. He had been riding here since he was young. Steve had always been a good friend to Robert.

"Robert, I'm so glad you took time to come ride today. We've missed you," Steve said.

"Robert's no fun anymore. Not since he got married," Gary said.

"Gary, will you cut it out? Robert made his choice. You need to accept it."

"Yeah, Gary. I swear. First you showed up in Maryland when I eloped. Then you constantly come over near the river where I live. Why don't you just accept that I married Sarah?"

"I think you just got married to get away from your crazy mom. Plus, you know you're different. You just won't admit who you really are," Gary said.

"I got married because I love Sarah and I want to have a family with her."

"Liar. You're not being honest with yourself."

"Gary, I'm happy with my decision and you need to accept it. I chose the lifestyle I wanted. You should choose it too. If you don't, you'll be thought of as weird or queer and you risk getting arrested if anyone finds out. If you wanted a chance to be free and happy with that other lifestyle, you'd need to go to New York City. I saw men like you hanging out together drinking and no one even cared."

"I'd love to move to New York City," Steve said, "But I'd sure have to have a really good job to be able to afford to live there."

"I am going to live there someday. I just need to save enough money to make it happen," Gary said.

"That's a good plan, Gary," Robert said. "You'd be happier there."

"I was happy here until my good friend decided to change course and get married."

"You knew I was going to get married."

"I didn't know it. I figured you just gave Sarah a ring as a cover. Then people wouldn't suspect anything. I didn't think you'd really do it."

"Will you two stop arguing? You sound like an old married couple. Let's go riding," Steve said. He got up on his horse. Robert was furious at Gary. He felt as though Gary was obsessed with him. He decided not to say anything because he thought Gary would just get more annoyed. Robert got up on his horse. The three men headed out onto the trails and rode in silence. Robert prayed Gary would just accept the choice he had made and move on.

Chapter 40

Sarah rushed home after work to make the coleslaw for the dinner at her mom's house. She couldn't wait to see Brenda. When she got home, Robert wasn't there. She wondered where he'd gone. It annoyed her.

She changed out of her work clothes and went into the kitchen. She turned on the radio and started shredding cabbage. She thought about becoming a mother. She was really getting excited about it. She couldn't wait to be a mom. She and Robert had started planning the nursery. They'd decided to paint it pale green. About twenty minutes later Sarah heard Robert come in through the front door.

"Hi, sweetie," Sarah called from the kitchen.

"Hey. How are you? How was work?" Robert asked as he walked over and gave Sarah a kiss on the cheek.

"It was busy but good. I helped out in the pharmacy area again today. How was your day?"

"Good. I took the afternoon off and went riding over at Steve's farm."

"You took the afternoon off? You're kidding, right?"

"We weren't busy at work and Steve called and asked me to go riding with him and Gary."

"Gary?" She gave Robert a glaring look. Now she was really perturbed.

"Yeah, Gary. You know he hangs out with Steve. Business is going great for Steve at his restaurant in Milltown. But he and Gary still aren't dating anyone seriously. They aren't lucky like me. I found the love of my life." Robert moved to kiss Sarah. She moved backwards.

"What's wrong with you?"

"Steve and Gary have never dated much. You know what people sometimes say about guys like that."

"No, what do they say?" Robert asked.

"That they're weird, different." She couldn't believe Robert had been riding. He had to get the nursery ready.

"I also stopped and saw my folks. Mom was drinking too much as usual and Dad was out working in the yard." *Does he bring his mom up for sympathy?* Sarah thought.

"I'm sorry. I know how much it bothers you when your mom drinks." Sarah went to the refrigerator and took out the mayonnaise.

"I'm used to it, unfortunately. She's done it most of my life." Robert drank the rest of his glass of milk. "I'll go get showered."

"Okay," Sarah replied. She was angry. He'd been off in the afternoon having fun rather than working on the nursery or doing things around the house. Here she was, pregnant, and she was working. Why did he always have to hang out with Steve and Gary? Maybe the pregnancy was making her temperamental. She finished making the coleslaw and then sat down to rest a little in the living room. Robert came out. Sarah jumped up.

"I just need to freshen up some," said Sarah. "Then we better go."

"You okay? You're acting strange today," Robert asked as they drove.

"I'm not the one who took the afternoon off. I'm just a little tired. That's all." Sarah couldn't wait to get into the bathroom and away from him. She went in the bathroom and shut the door. She turned on the water so he couldn't hear her and burst into tears.

"Well, hi there, Sarah and Robert. Long time no see. I hear congratulations are in order." Joe walked up and shook Robert's hand. He then gave Sarah a kiss on the cheek.

"Thanks, Uncle Joe." Sarah suddenly felt a little happier.

"How are you feeling?" Uncle Joe asked as he walked Sarah into the house.

"Pretty good actually. I'm not as tired as I was the first few weeks," Sarah replied. Robert followed behind them.

"Sarah, Sarah," Brenda raced up to Sarah, gave her a big hug, and took the coleslaw. "Oh, Sarah, I missed you. I so wished I could have talked to you from England."

"Why, did something go wrong?" Sarah asked, looking concerned.

"No, no, the exact opposite. Check this out." Brenda put her left hand out. Sarah saw the ring sparkle in the light. The diamond was beautiful and bigger than her own.

"Wow. Oh my gosh, you got engaged. Congratulations. The ring is gorgeous." Sarah eyed the ring with a touch of jealousy even though she was happy for her sister.

"Well, congratulations, Brenda." Robert came up from behind and put his arm around her shoulders.

"Oh, Robert. You're here?" Brenda looked confused.

"Yes, I am. The feud is over," he whispered. Sarah overheard and smiled even though she was still angry at Robert. She couldn't figure out why Robert hadn't told her in the morning that he was going riding with Steve and Gary. She didn't believe Steve had called Robert at work to ask him.

"Why is the feud over? What changed?" Brenda asked.

"I'm going to have a baby." Sarah patted her stomach. For the first time in a long time, Sarah saw that Brenda was speechless.

Chapter 41

When Sarah arrived for her shift, Gus was up front talking with Hazel while he bought his paper.

"Well, hey there, Sarah, I heard congratulations are in order," Gus said.

"Thanks, Gus. We're super excited."

"When are you due?"

"In about five months, so I have a long way to go."

"Well, I'm happy for you."

"It sure will be a beautiful baby if it gets its mom's looks," Hazel said.

"Thanks guys." Sarah felt a little down. She couldn't wait to be a mom but she was having doubts about married life. It still bothered her that Robert had taken a half day off from work to hang out with Gary and Steve and hadn't told her beforehand. And that had been a couple of weeks ago, what else hadn't he told her?

"Good morning, Sarah," Laura said.

"Hi there, Laura."

"Guess what?" Laura had a huge smile on her face.

"What?"

"We hired Richard as the new pharmacist. His references were outstanding. Henry wanted to hire the older gentleman but there was just something about Richard that I really liked. I convinced Henry to hire him. He starts today."

"Wow. He sure is a nice-looking man. Heather will be happy we hired him," Sarah said.

"Hired who?" Heather said as she walked back to the pharmacy area. She'd just arrived.

"Richard. Laura hired Richard."

"Well, alright. Not only is he cute but he seemed liked a super nice guy. Plus, he finished pharmacy school recently so he can give me pointers on applying." Heather patted Sarah on the back.

"Luckily there are no customers in here," Hazel said, approaching them. "You three sound like a bunch of hens back here. What time does the new guy start?"

"Eleven o'clock." Laura counted out pills for a prescription.

"Well, I can't wait to watch this," Hazel said.

Chapter 42

At eleven o'clock, Richard came through the front door. He was wearing a white shirt, blue trousers, and a dark blue tie. He must have been to the beach because he had an amazing tan. Richard waved at Heather then walked towards the pharmacy area. Heather saw him say hello to Sarah as he walked by the soda fountain where she was pouring coffee. Richard continued to the pharmacy area and stopped in front of Heather. Heather just stared at him. She'd never felt this tongue-tied before. She spotted Sarah watching her from the soda fountain, chuckling.

"Hi! I'm Richard, the new pharmacist. I think I met you when I interviewed." Richard reached out his hand. This took Heather out of her trance.

"Yes, hi, I'm Heather. I work in the soda fountain and I help back here in the pharmacy. I hope to go to pharmacy school one day. I take courses at Milltown Community College." Heather shook his hand.

"Well, good for you. I went to the University of Connecticut and graduated last year so if you have any questions, just let me know." Richard smiled warmly at Heather. Heather felt herself blushing. She thought he was one of the most gorgeous men she had ever seen.

"Hi there, Richard," Laura said. "I see you met Heather again. Okay, Heather, you can move over to the soda fountain and help Sarah prepare for the lunch crowd. Richard and I will work back here."

"Sure thing," Heather replied. She smiled as she walked past Richard. She brushed against him accidently. Her body felt electrified. She was surprised at her reaction.

Heather hadn't dated much. She considered herself a nerd. She spent most of her free time working or taking classes. She really wanted to be a pharmacist and she had to work to pay her way through school. Richard might be the most good-looking man she had ever seen but Dylan was the nicest. And Dylan was cute too. She tried to focus her thoughts on Dylan. He was good to her. She felt guilty about her reaction to Richard.

Chapter 43

renda hung up the kitchen phone. She was devastated. Tears streamed down her face. She turned her back to her mother so she couldn't see her crying.

"What's the matter?" Elizabeth asked.

"It's Harry. His leave got cancelled. They've been busier than usual because of the war in Vietnam so he needs to stay on base right now." Brenda grabbed a napkin and blew her nose.

"Oh dear. I'm so sorry. Did you get any sense of when you will see him again?"

"Not really. He asked if I could come to visit him in England in a couple of months. His parents will be visiting him again." Brenda sat down at the kitchen table.

"Well, that sounds like a plan. What do you think of that?" Elizabeth put two hot chocolate chip cookies on a plate in front of Brenda. She poured each of them a glass of milk.

"I'd love to visit England again. I really enjoyed being on the base. Mrs. Singer was lots of fun to stay with."

"Well then, try to focus on that."

"I know, Mom," Brenda blew her nose again. "I just really miss him a lot. We were going to look at places to have the wedding. Now I need to wait until he's granted leave."

"Well, you could go look at places to have the wedding

without him. Sarah loves that kind of stuff." Elizabeth took a sip of milk.

"That's an idea. I didn't think of that. I just so wanted to see Harry." Brenda started crying again.

"Oh dear, dear, it'll be fine."

"Thanks, Mom. I'm going to go for a walk to clear my mind." Brenda grabbed the other cookie and gave her mom a kiss on the top of her head.

"Think about what I said. Get Sarah to go look at wedding venues with you. It'll cheer you up."

"I'll think about it, Mom." She needed to pull herself together, but she started crying as she walked downstairs. When she got to the bottom of the landing, she ran into Teddy.

"Hi there, Brenda. What's wrong?" Teddy asked.

"Oh, don't mind me. I'm just feeling sorry for myself because Harry's leave got cancelled so now I have to wait another two months to see him." Brenda dried her tears with the messy napkin in her hand.

"I'm sorry, Brenda. That must be real tough on Harry as well. Imagine you think you're coming home to see your girl and you're suddenly told you can't." Teddy followed Brenda outside.

"Good point, Teddy. I guess I should think of it from his point of view too," Brenda said.

"I heard the war is heating up. Our friend Vinny is in Vietnam right now. He wrote me a letter and said the fighting is pretty intense where he is. Luckily Harry is on an air base in England. At least he's somewhat safe."

"You're right, Teddy. It could be worse. Where are you headed?"

"Down to the pharmacy to get a milkshake. Want to walk with me?"

"Sure."

"What are you two doing here?" Heather asked.

"I'm here for a chocolate shake and my friend here needs some cheering up." Teddy smiled at Heather. He and Brenda sat down at the counter.

"What's wrong, Brenda?" Heather asked as she scooped out ice cream for Teddy's shake.

"I just found out Harry's leave got cancelled. I'm bummed."

"Oh no. Dylan said you were so excited that he was coming next week." Heather poured milk into the cup with the chocolate ice cream.

"It's awful but Teddy made me realize that Harry is probably even more bummed since he has to work and can't come home."

"Well, can I make you a root beer float? I know you love them. Drown your sorrows in ice cream."

"Might as well. Thanks Heather." Brenda looked back toward the pharmacy. She spotted Sarah on the phone. Brenda couldn't believe how pregnant Sarah looked. They had gone shopping together for maternity clothes a few weeks ago. Brenda spotted a handsome young man back there with Sarah.

"Hey, who's the man back there with Sarah?"

"Oh, that's Richard. He's the new pharmacist." Heather put Teddy's chocolate shake down in front of him. Teddy turned to see who Brenda and Heather were talking about.

"He's handsome," Brenda said.

"He sure is and he's a very nice man too."

"Is he married?" Teddy asked.

"Nope and he doesn't have a girlfriend either," Heather answered.

"Well, I bet there are plenty of young women in this town who would like to change that," Brenda said.

"Ain't that the truth," Teddy said. "There are not enough single men in this town to go around."

"What are you guys doing here?" Sarah asked.

"Harry's leave got cancelled," Brenda said. Tears fell down her cheek. She tried to wipe them away before anyone could see.

"Oh, sis. I'm so sorry. How did that happen?"

"He called to tell me. They're super busy with everything right now so all leaves were cancelled."

"Oh no. Have you thought about going back over there to visit him?"

"He mentioned that maybe I could come in a couple months when his parents go visit."

"Well, that's a fabulous idea. Focus on that."

"And Mom said I should ask you to visit wedding venues with me."

"I'd love that, Brenda, especially since I never got to do that."

Chapter 44

"You want to drive or you want me to?" Sarah asked.
"I'll drive," Brenda said. "Shall we go look at the barn first?"

"Oh, that would be neat," Sarah said.

"Well, I heard you could have a wedding at the barn." Brenda turned toward Milltown.

"That would be fun. Plus, a lot of Harry's family is from Milltown."

"I sure miss him, Sarah. It's tough not seeing him for such long periods of time."

"I know it must be tough. But didn't you say you're going over there again soon?"

"Yes. In a few weeks, with his parents."

"Well, focus on that then. Do you know how much some girls would die to be able to go to England even once?" Sarah asked. "You're so lucky."

"That's a good point. I'll stop feeling sorry for myself." Brenda looked over at Sarah. "How you feeling anyway?"

"I'm feeling good. Nothing as bad as the first trimester. I'm just getting so big that it's tough to sleep at night." Sarah opened her purse and took out a mint.

"How's Robert taking all this?" Brenda asked.

"He says he's excited. He doesn't seem to have a lot of interest in me though, you know, sexually, ever since I got pregnant."

Brenda thought that was odd. She'd always heard that men usually wanted sex regardless. However, she didn't want to stress out her pregnant sister. "Ahh, sis, you worry too much. You're pregnant. He'll be right back at you once you have the baby."

"I guess I do worry too much. Hey, turn there, it's a sign for the barn." Brenda turned fast to the right. They followed the road towards the barn. The road was lined with gorgeous flower beds and grassy walkways on each side. Birds darted between the flower beds. A large red barn was set back from the road.

"Wow, this is so pretty," Brenda said as they drove to the barn. "I've never been back here before."

"Me neither. Been by this road quite a bit but never on it." Sarah gazed at the flower gardens. "I love the flowers."

"How was the place where you got married?" Brenda asked, as she pulled into a parking place.

"It was a nice old stone house, but nothing like this."

"Wow, this is much fancier than I thought." Brenda eyed the birdbaths in the gardens.

"It'll be fun to check it out." Sarah pulled open the front door.

Brenda followed her in. The place was gorgeous; rustic-looking but tastefully decorated with beautiful lighting. The room was filled with antique furniture and vases of fresh cut flowers. A woman sat at a desk facing them.

"May I help you?"

"Yes, hi. We're looking at different wedding venues today to get a sense of what's available in the area," Brenda said.

"Well, welcome. I'm Harriett and I'd be happy to help you." The woman stood up and handed Brenda a brochure. "Here's some information on the barn. Let me ask you some questions so I can help figure out your needs. When do you plan to get married?"

"Hopefully sometime next summer."

"Do you plan to have the ceremony here or just the reception?"

"Just the reception."

"About how many guests?"

"Well, ahhh, maybe a hundred. Harry has a large family."

"That answers my other question, so Harry is your fiancé?" Brenda was starting to get annoyed at all the questions.

"Yes, my fiancé's name is Harry Rigoni and he's in the air force in England right now," Brenda said. "Can we walk around and see everything?"

"Sure," Harriett said. She walked them back into the barn area. There was a large fireplace and tables set up throughout the room, and a large dance floor on the right. The windows overlooked the meticulously decorated grounds and a lake with swans.

"You thinking of having a disc jockey or band?" Harriett asked.

"Hadn't even thought about it yet," Brenda replied. "What's most common?"

"Typically, a disc jockey. And we have terrific food, you can do buffet or a sit-down meal. In the brochure I gave you there are all the possible options with the prices. Let's walk outside and you can check out the lake."

Brenda and Sarah followed the woman outside. Brenda wondered why Sarah was being so quiet. It wasn't like her. She was smiling and following Brenda and the woman around, but not really saying anything. Harriett walked them over to the gazebo on the lake. The swans and ducks swam up to them, thinking that they were going to throw them food.

"This is a perfect spot for photos. Do you have any sense of what date you're looking at?"

"Not yet," Brenda said, "with him being in the military."

"I know, I know. Unfortunately, I see a lot of that. But now you have the basic information. If you have any questions as you read through the materials, just give me a call."

"Well, thank you very much." Brenda stopped and shook Harriet's hand. "We very much appreciate your time."

"Yes, thank you." Sarah shook her hand too. Harriett headed back to the barn while Brenda and Sarah walked down the path toward the parking lot.

When Harriett was out of earshot, Sarah said, "What did she mean by, we see a lot of that?"

"I don't know," Brenda said. "Why were you so quiet?"

"I was just overwhelmed at how fancy this all was. I guess I figured because it was called a barn, that it wouldn't be so high end."

"I know. We can't afford something like this. If the bride's parents are supposed to fund the wedding then this place is out, because I don't have this kind of money and Mom and Dad don't either."

"That was the one positive thing about me eloping; it didn't cost the family anything."

Chapter 45

Heather spotted Brenda as she walked into the pharmacy. It was about fifteen minutes before closing. As soon as Heather was done with work, she and Brenda were going to go to the pizza place to plan Sarah's baby shower.

"Love your dress," Heather said as Brenda sat down at the soda fountain.

"Thanks, Heather. Kind of quiet right now, huh?" Brenda looked around. She saw Richard working in the back and no one was up front.

"Yeah, just me and Richard. Hazel asked if she could leave early because she's going bowling with some friends. I've been covering up front and back here. I'm just getting everything in order here for tomorrow morning." Heather washed out a glass.

"Well, thanks for being willing to plan this with me. Dylan told me to tell you hello. He was heading over to Teddy's to watch some game on television."

"Those two. They could watch sports all day," Heather said. She eyed Richard walking over to them.

"What's all the laughter over here?"

"Richard, this is Sarah's sister, Brenda, and Brenda, this is Richard, our new pharmacist." Heather wiped down the counter.

"Well, nice to meet you Brenda. I've heard a lot about you." Richard shook Brenda's hand. Brenda turned a little red. *He is cute,* Brenda thought. Brenda saw Heather chuckle to herself and turn back to grab another glass to wash.

"Nice to meet you, Richard. I've heard a lot about you too," Brenda said. "Where are you from?"

"I'm from Robinsville. I went to pharmacy school up at UCONN and graduated last year. I was working up at Milltown Hospital, but I always wanted to work in a community pharmacy so here I am. What are you two up to?"

"We're heading over to the pizza place to plan a baby shower for Sarah," Heather replied. "How about you, Richard? What are you doing after work?"

"My family's having a get together at my aunt's house so I'm heading over there. My cousin's heading off to England next week. He's going over to an air force base over there. He's a pilot." Richard sat down next to Brenda.

"Oh, what base?" Brenda asked, "My fiancé is over at Alconbury. I was just over there a few months ago."

"No way. My cousin is going to Alconbury," Richard said. "Is he a pilot too?"

"No, he's an engineer, he works on the planes' radars," Brenda said.

"Well, if my cousin has any questions about Alconbury, can he give you a call?"

"Sure." Brenda grabbed a napkin and took a pen out of her purse. She wrote down her phone number and handed the napkin to Richard. Brenda thought Heather looked jealous but wasn't quite sure why. Maybe all women just wanted Richard to have their phone number. Now that Richard had Brenda's number, he could call her anytime. But it didn't matter, she was engaged.

"Thanks, I appreciate this," Richard said, holding up the napkin. "Guess we better lock up this place and get out of here. Heather, if you grab all the register drawers and put them in the safe then I can count them all tomorrow."

"Okay."

"Ready to go?" Brenda got up from the soda fountain as Heather walked towards her.

"I sure am, I'm hungry," Heather said as they walked together to the front door.

"Here, let me let you two out." Richard walked up to unlock the front door. "Nice to meet you, Brenda. See you around."

Brenda and Heather walked out to the parking lot and got into Heather's car.

"Isn't Richard handsome?" Heather said as she started the car.

"He sure is."

"He's going to be a good catch for some woman." Heather turned out of the pharmacy parking lot onto Main Street.

"He must have a girlfriend. He's handsome and he has a good job." Brenda looked at Heather.

"No, from what I have heard he's pretty serious. He's super smart and he does a lot with his family."

"Well then, maybe we need to invite him to the shower so he can meet more people," Brenda said.

"Great idea."

Chapter 46

Elizabeth was excited. She, Abbey, and Mrs. Smith were decorating the pool area for Sarah's baby shower. They were hanging green streamers and white Christmas tree lights along the fence. Dylan and Teddy were in the garage looking for folding tables and chairs to bring to the pool area. Heather and Brenda had gone down to the local store to buy bags of ice for the coolers. Eugene, Joe, and Dr. Smith were setting up the grill right outside the pool area so that they could cook hot dogs and hamburgers.

"Oh, this is so much fun." Mrs. Smith plugged in the lights to test them. "Oh, it looks so pretty."

"Well, thanks so much for helping with all of this." Elizabeth opened another bag of streamers.

"I'm so excited. You beat me in becoming a grandmother but it will be fun having young children around again," Mrs. Smith said.

"Man, these are heavy." Teddy helped Dylan carry a table over.

"You two are the manly labor," Abbey said as she set up the cake table. Abbey had made a multi-level cake decorated with *Congratulations Robert and Sarah* and a light green baby carriage. Elizabeth thought it was gorgeous. Abbey and Joe were amazing bakers.

"Come on, Teddy, we got two more tables to bring out." Dylan walked back towards the garage. Elizabeth was glad they'd rented the place above the Smiths. They were wonderful landlords and they had become close friends. Elizabeth especially had enjoyed watching Dylan and Teddy's friendship over the years.

"I'm coming." Teddy followed Dylan towards the garage. "You're killing me."

Elizabeth, Heather, and Brenda had gathered earlier in Elizabeth's kitchen to make all the salads for the party. Brenda had bought all the ingredients and stored them at Heather's place so Sarah wouldn't get suspicious. They'd made potato salad, coleslaw, and deviled eggs. Elizabeth had enjoyed it. Heather was growing on her. She was glad Dylan and Heather were getting along so well.

"Hi guys," Dylan said as Heather and Brenda got out of Brenda's car.

"Thanks for getting this, now we can ice down the coolers and put the meat into them and then start cooking." Eugene lifted a bag of ice from the trunk. Dylan gave Heather a kiss. Elizabeth loved to see how Heather beamed whenever Dylan was around. Elizabeth could also tell that Brenda was really missing Harry. His leave being cancelled had knocked the wind out of her but planning the shower with Heather had been a great distraction.

Joe and Dr. Smith walked past with bags of ice which they poured over the beer and soft drinks that were in the coolers. When Elizabeth finished hanging the streamers, she went inside to get the white tablecloths and flowers for the table. She and Brenda had filled small vases with wildflowers. The blue, white, purple, and yellow flowers looked gorgeous. Elizabeth picked up the box of flowers.

"Here, Mom let me get that." Brenda took the box from her mother. "You grab the tablecloths."

"Brenda, you and Heather have done such a wonderful job planning the shower."

"Thanks, Mom. It's been fun. Now when I have a baby down the road, you guys have to top this." They walked to the pool area and decorated all the tables. Then Elizabeth and Brenda set up a buffet table. Brenda had bought cute paper plates with yellow and purple flowers on them. She decorated a card table with a light green tablecloth and put a basket on top of it. This would be the gift table.

Elizabeth went back inside and got the pitchers of lemonade. She brought them out to the buffet table. "Come on, Brenda, let's take a break before the guests start arriving."

"Sounds good." Brenda came over and filled two paper cups with ice. Elizabeth poured lemonade into both of them. They sat down in some pool chairs. Abbey came outside with more pitchers of lemonade and Mrs. Smith followed with iced tea. They poured themselves drinks and joined them.

"Let's start cooking, Eugene." Dr. Smith doused the charcoal with lighter fluid.

"You got it." Eugene lit a match and started the fire. Elizabeth loved the warmth of fires.

Joe went over to the coolers and grabbed three beers and brought them over to the grill. "Here you go. They'll help us cook better."

"You guys always have a good excuse for beer," Abbey said.

Robert's parents, Thomas and Mary arrived. Mary was carrying a large bowl of fruit salad and Thomas had a watermelon.

"Welcome, welcome." Elizabeth stood and walked over to greet them. She gave them each a kiss on the cheek.

"Where should we put this stuff?" Mary asked.

"Here, come with me and we'll put it in the fridge. Thomas, why don't you go have a beer with the guys at the grill?" Elizabeth took the watermelon from Thomas.

"I can't pass that up." Thomas gave Elizabeth a kiss on

the cheek. She and Mary went into the house and put the fruit salad in the refrigerator.

"Thanks so much for throwing this for them. I can't wait until we're grandmothers," Mary said.

"Don't thank me, this is Heather and Brenda's great planning." Elizabeth put the watermelon on a cutting board and took a knife off a rack. "Let's cut this up."

"I have four blueberry pies in the car. Do you mind if I go get them?" Mary asked.

"Not at all. I love your blueberry pie and so does Sarah. What a nice surprise." Elizabeth cut the watermelon in half. Elizabeth liked Mary as best as she could but she knew that her drinking haunted Robert which then impacted Sarah. Several minutes later, Robert came through the back door with two of his mother's pies.

"Robert, dear. I'm so glad you are here." Elizabeth cut slices of watermelon. "Just throw the pies on the counter and come give me a hug."

Robert smiled and walked over and hugged Elizabeth. "Thanks so much for doing this. Sarah is going to be so surprised."

"I'm so happy for you both. You'll make great parents." Elizabeth rubbed Robert's arm.

"I'm extremely excited. I'm looking forward to being a dad. Can't wait to see if it's a boy or girl. Well, I better go get the other two pies."

"What happened to your mom? I thought she was getting them."

"When she saw me arrive she asked if I could get the pies out of their car. She went right for the wine." *That woman,* Elizabeth thought.

Chapter 47

Sarah was exhausted but she'd promised her mom she would stop by to help with the canning that she and Brenda were doing. She picked up the bag of old clothes that she would change into at her mom's house.

"Have a good night, Sarah. Doing anything special?" Richard asked.

"Nope. Just going to help my mother with some canning. How about you?"

"Not really. After I close up in a half hour I'm heading home. Since I have to work tomorrow, I'm just going to get some rest and relaxation tonight."

"Well, have a good evening, I'll lock you in." Sarah turned and walked toward the front of the store.

"You too," Richard called as Sarah walked up front. The night air was cool. The farther she walked, the more awake she became. She felt the baby kick. The baby liked the walking too. She couldn't wait to have the baby; she wondered if it would be a boy or girl. Robert had finished painting the nursery light green and they had hung the curtains. His mom and dad were giving them the crib. They'd picked it out last weekend with them. The crib was white and it came with a matching white dresser. Sarah's mood had been up and down with the pregnancy.

Sarah breathed in the fresh air. She passed the Millers' house. The family waved from across the street as she walked by. She loved this town. She knew just about everyone from working at the pharmacy. Sarah wished she wanted to pursue a pharmacy degree like Heather but she really didn't have the ambition to do it. Her priority was to have several children and to continue working part-time at the pharmacy. As Sarah walked towards her mother's house, she noticed that there were lots of cars parked outside. Maybe the Smiths were having a get together.

Suddenly, Sarah noticed her mom, Robert, Brenda, Heather, and Dylan walking toward her. She couldn't figure out why they were all there.

"Surprise, surprise," they said. Brenda came up to her and grabbed the bag of clothes out of her hand.

"What's going on?" Sarah asked.

"This is your baby shower, baby sister." Dylan took a photo of her with a confused look on her face. Robert put his arm around her.

"Come on down to your guests." Heather motioned for Sarah and Robert to follow her as she strolled down the hill. Sarah couldn't believe all the people who were down at the Smiths' pool. Even Hazel, who had left the pharmacy just thirty minutes before Sarah, was sitting by the pool sipping a glass of lemonade. Sarah's eyes glistened with tears of happiness.

"Surprise," the crowd yelled. Sarah couldn't believe the pool area. White lights and green streamers lined the fences. Vases of flowers sat on top of tables with white tablecloths. Eugene, Joe, and Dr. Smith were cooking burgers and hot dogs on the grill. Robert's parents sat at a table next to the grill.

"Sarah, dear. Congratulations. I told your mother that I'd be fighting her to watch the baby. You can call on me anytime."

"I may take you up on that." Sarah wiped a tear from

the corner of her eye. Sarah noticed her mom placing her arm around Robert. She enjoyed watching her mom dote on Robert. Their friendship had returned to what it had been before Robert and Sarah had eloped.

"Come on, let's eat everyone," Eugene called. "The burgers and hot dogs are calling."

They started moving toward the buffet table. Sarah walked over to pour herself some lemonade while Robert made his way over to make himself a plate of food. After Sarah poured herself a drink she walked over to Hazel. "Going to a surprise party, huh?"

"Hey, a girl has to do what a girl has to do," Hazel said. "Richard is in on this too. He's coming as soon as he shuts down the pharmacy."

"He is? Who invited him?"

"Heather and I did," Brenda said. "I met Richard one night when I met up with Heather when she got off of work. What a nice man, and he speaks highly of you so I figured why not invite him. You don't mind, do you?"

"Of course not." Sarah wondered what her sister was up to. Sarah saw Beth, and some other friends from high school. She watched Robert's mother drinking wine. Watching his mother infuriated her. Why couldn't the woman avoid drinking too much at parties? It caused Robert great pain and embarrassment.

Sarah felt a tap on her shoulder. She turned and saw Richard. "Richard. Thanks so much for coming. Brenda just told me she'd invited you."

"It was hard acting like I wasn't doing anything tonight."

"Are you going to introduce us?" Sarah's friend Beth asked. Women loved Richard. Sarah chuckled to herself as she went to find Robert. She spotted him going into the house with Dylan. Sarah tried to catch up to them but she moved very slowly. When she walked into the kitchen, she overheard Robert and Dylan talking.

"Dylan. You don't have to worry about Richard. He just works with Heather."

"What are you two talking about?" Sarah asked.

"Dylan's a little jealous of Richard. Heather is down there talking with him. Check it out." Heather was standing close to Richard; they were deep in conversation. Sarah's high school friends had gone to the buffet table to get food.

"Don't be jealous of Richard. Every single woman in this town likes to talk to him. We just need to find him a woman so he can settle down." Sarah continued to watch Heather and Richard from the window.

Chapter 48

Dylan was peering through his books. He had a final exam in accounting methods in two days. He looked up and saw Teddy walking across the library lobby towards him. Teddy didn't look quite right to Dylan. Something must be wrong.

"What's up?"

"Come on with me. I need to talk with you about something."

"Now? I thought you had a final you had to study for?"

"Yes, now. Come on. I don't want to make a scene in here." Teddy grabbed some of Dylan's books to carry. Dylan picked up his notebooks and paper. He followed Teddy towards the door and then outside into the quad.

"What's wrong, Teddy?"

"Not here, Dylan. Let's go down to the pizza place." They walked in silence. Dylan had never seen Teddy like this. He wondered if Teddy and Amber had broken up or if something had happened to Teddy's mom or dad. Teddy opened the door to the pizza place and motioned for Dylan to walk in.

"Table for two," Dylan said to the hostess.

"Can it be over in that corner?" Teddy pointed.

"Sure. Follow me." The hostess took two menus and walked toward the corner table. Teddy and Dylan followed and sat down at the booth. The waitress handed them the menus.

"Can I get you something to drink?"

"Two beers please, Schaefer if you have it," Teddy said.

"You got it." The hostess went to get them the beers.

"Beer, now? We got exams," Dylan said.

"Vinny's dead."

"What?" Dylan stared at Teddy in shock.

"Vinny's dead. He got killed in Vietnam. His sister called to tell me. The funeral is in a few days." Teddy put his face in his hands. Dylan didn't know what to say. He'd been friends with Vinny since kindergarten. His eyes welled up with tears.

"How?"

"Shot by a sniper." Teddy wiped his face. The hostess put the beers down on the table. She must have sensed something was wrong because she quickly hurried away.

"Oh God, Teddy, I'm sure going to miss him."

"I sure am going to miss him too. He was supposed to come home on leave in a few weeks." Teddy shook his head.

"How did his sister sound?" Dylan asked.

"A mess," Teddy replied. "And can you imagine how Kelly feels?"

"They were supposed to get married next summer."

"This war is a mess. It makes me want to enlist even sooner than I planned to."

"I know what you mean. Part of me really wants to join the navy. This makes me want to do it even more than ever." Dylan took a sip of his beer.

"Me too, I want to serve our country and they need our help." Teddy raised his beer glass "Here's to Vinny. May he rest in peace."

Dylan clinked Teddy's glass. "May he rest in peace."

Chapter 49

Heather placed a prescription label on the vial. She'd just filled Mrs. Jones' thyroid medication. She was working next to Richard who picked up the prescription to check it. Mrs. Jones was impatiently pacing in the pharmacy.

"Here you go, Mrs. Jones," Richard called as he walked over to the counter. "Do you have any questions about the medication?"

"I certainly do not. I've been on it forever."

"Good to see you, Mrs. Jones." Richard smiled as Mrs. Jones turned to hurry out of the pharmacy. Heather giggled.

"How are your classes going?" Richard asked.

"They're good, except chemistry is quite tough. I have one of the hardest teachers and he's not good at explaining things."

"Well, I was actually pretty good at chemistry. If you ever want some help, just let me know."

"I'd love your help," Heather said. "We have a big test next week."

"Well, want to meet up after work for dinner and I can help you? We both get off at five." Heather thought about it; Dylan was tied up with his own studying for finals tonight. Plus, he had been acting very aloof since he'd found out about Vinny. Heather felt terrible for Dylan, but she wasn't quite sure how to console him.

"Sure. That would be great."

"How about we meet at the Chinese restaurant at six. Just bring your books."

"Sounds good to me, Richard. I really appreciate it."

"Hi there," Richard called. He took the books Heather was carrying.

"Hi Richard." Heather smiled widely. "Thanks again for helping me."

"No problem." Richard and Heather walked into the Chinese restaurant. Richard ordered a couple of dishes for them to share. Heather opened the books and showed Richard the chapter she was having trouble with. Richard thought Heather was one of the most gorgeous women he had ever met. He hadn't been much of a dater in college. Women always flirted with him, but it made him uncomfortable. Heather made him feel at ease.

They ate egg rolls in between talking about the chemistry questions. Richard loved teaching and Heather picked things up easily. Suddenly Heather's face became white. Richard turned and saw a man and a woman walking towards their booth, following the hostess. Richard remembered meeting them at Sarah's shower but he couldn't remember their names.

"Hi Teddy, hi Amber." Heather stopped eating as they walked by.

"Well, look here. Hi guys. What are you two up to?" Teddy gave Heather a puzzled look.

"Richard's helping me study for my chemistry test." Heather smiled sheepishly.

"Where's Dylan?" Amber asked.

"Studying for his finals," Heather answered.

"Well, have fun," Teddy said. He and Amber continued

following the hostess. Richard saw Teddy roll his eyes at Amber as they left.

"Teddy is Dylan's best friend. I guess he was surprised to see us here together." Richard could tell she was stressed.

"Well, I'm a pharmacist helping a future pharmacist. Nothing wrong with that."

"That's very true. I think both Teddy and Dylan are super sensitive right now. They lost a good friend recently in the war."

"Oh no, that is too bad. I've lost friends too. It's terrible."

Chapter 50

Robert woke up startled. The phone was ringing. It was ten thirty. No one ever called this late. He jumped up and ran to get the phone before it woke Sarah.

"Hello."

"Robert, this is Ray from the fire department. There's been a fire are your parents' place. They're fine. Your dad wanted me to call. Can you come by?"

"Oh God. Are you sure they're okay?"

"Yes, yes, but please come by as soon as you can," Ray said. Robert raced into the bedroom to dress.

"What's wrong? Are you okay?" Sarah asked.

"There's been a fire at my parents' place. I need to go over there."

"Let me go with you," Sarah said as she got out of bed.

"No, no. A fire is not where a pregnant woman should be. You stay here. I'll call to let you know what's going on," Robert said. He kissed Sarah and then rushed out of the door. His heart was racing. He drove as fast as he could to his parents' place.

There were fire trucks everywhere. He smelled smoke. He stopped the car and walked toward the scene. The firemen were still hosing down the building. Smoke was rising from the burning home. He saw his parents' neighbors out watching the horrific scene. He went up to a fireman and said, "I'm Robert. This is my parents' place. Do you know where they are?"

"Your mom was taken to the hospital for smoke inhalation, but your dad is over at that ambulance," the fireman said.

"Dad, Dad. Are you alright?" His dad was sitting on the back of the ambulance hooked up to oxygen.

"I'm okay, son. Just some smoke inhalation. They've been taking good care of me," Thomas said.

"What about Mom?"

"She should be fine. She suffered a lot more smoke inhalation than me and minor burns. They took her to Milltown Hospital."

"What started the fire?"

"They think your mom fell asleep and her cigarette caught the bedding on fire," Thomas said. Robert knew that meant she had been drinking and smoking in bed and she must have passed out. It took all of Robert's effort to not say anything in anger. What was wrong with his mother? Did she ever think of anyone but herself? She was such an embarrassment.

"I was in the living room watching television and I smelled smoke. I went back and saw the flames. I grabbed your mom and carried her out of the house. I ran over to Michael's and asked him to call the fire department."

"You sure you're okay, Dad?" Robert said. He sat down next to his dad.

"Yes, I am. I don't think the house is though," his dad said. Robert scanned the house to assess the damage. It looked as though the bedrooms were destroyed.

"It'll be okay, Dad," Robert said. The whole situation was overwhelming.

"You ready to head to the hospital?" the paramedic asked Thomas.

"Hospital?" Robert asked.

"We need to take your dad in to check him out. He refused to go until you got here," the paramedic said. "You can ride up front with me."

The paramedics got his dad strapped in and comfortable in the back of the ambulance. One paramedic sat next to his dad. Robert got into the front of the ambulance. Robert realized his dad might not be as in good shape as he thought.

Robert cradled his head in his hands. His head hurt. He was exhausted. Both his mom and dad were being evaluated in the emergency room. His mom was still incoherent due to smoke inhalation and her blood alcohol level. Robert felt guilty that sometimes he just wished she would die. She was such an embarrassment. Now she had destroyed his parents' home. He felt a hand on his shoulder. He looked up.

"Oh God, I am so happy to see you," Robert said. He got up and embraced Sarah. She was his rock. He didn't know what he'd do without her.

"I am so sorry, Robert, are you okay?"

"I'm just emotionally exhausted. They're going to keep them both overnight to observe them. Raymond's already driving down from Vermont to help," Robert said.

"How's the house?"

"It's a wreck. An absolute wreck," Robert said. "Raymond and I are going to have to find them an apartment to stay in."

"They can stay with us," Sarah said.

"No, not with the baby coming. It would be too crowded. You don't need extra stress. Don't worry. It'll be okay," Robert said.

"Have you eaten breakfast?"

"No."

"Let's go get something. It might make you feel better," Sarah said. She put her arm around him and they walked down the hallway. He was so glad she was there. He'd be lost without her. Ever since Sarah had questioned the sexuality of Gary and Steve, Robert had stopped hanging out with them. He couldn't jeopardize his relationship with Sarah.

Chapter 51

Elizabeth sat at the kitchen table reading the newspaper. Babs the cat rubbed against her legs. Elizabeth bent down to pet Babs. Brenda came into the kitchen, grabbed a mug from the cupboard, and poured herself some coffee. "What you reading, Mom?"

"Unfortunately, an article about a boy in the next town over that was killed in the war. It makes me so sad to see how many young men are getting killed."

"I know. I can't even imagine how Vinny's fiancé feels. I still can't believe he's dead. Dylan told me that his funeral was rough."

"Dylan does seem quite broken up about it." Elizabeth put down the newspaper. "Let me get more coffee."

"Here, I'll pour you some."

Suddenly there was a knock on the back door.

"Who on earth is that?" Elizabeth asked. She got up and opened the back door. "Teddy. What are you doing up so early on a Saturday?"

"Good morning, Mrs. Jones. Just looking for Dylan." Teddy scanned the room. "Hi there, Brenda."

"Hey, Teddy. Want some coffee? Come join us."

"I have time for a cup. Is Dylan still sleeping?"

"Nope. He's out fishing with Dad." Brenda put on a fresh pot of coffee. She then put some oatmeal cookies on a plate and brought them over to the table.

"Those sure look good." Teddy eyed the cookies.

"Go ahead and have one," Elizabeth said.

"You sure are an awesome cook, Mrs. Jones." Teddy took a cookie and bit into it.

"What are you up to today, Teddy?" Elizabeth asked.

"I'm heading into Milltown to do some shopping and I just wanted to see if Dylan wanted to come along. But I'm glad Dylan's out fishing. He needs a distraction. Between Vinny's death and Heather, it's been a tough week," Teddy said.

"Heather? What's wrong with Heather?" Brenda asked.

"It seems as though the new pharmacist in town is after her." Teddy raised his eyebrows.

"You're kidding," Brenda said. "Richard doesn't seem that way to me. He wouldn't do that to Dylan."

"Well, Amber and I saw Heather out with Richard having Chinese food." Teddy put a spoonful of sugar into his coffee. Brenda and Elizabeth locked eyes.

"Oh no," Elizabeth said.

"What's wrong?" Teddy asked.

"Look at this picture. Oh no," Elizabeth said. Brenda picked up the newspaper. Her heart sank. It was Robert's parents' place. Half the house was destroyed.

"What's wrong?" Teddy asked.

"There was a fire last night. It was Robert's parents' house." Elizabeth said. Brenda held the paper up so Teddy could see it.

"Oh no. Did they say what started it?" Teddy asked. Brenda scanned the article.

"No."

"I bet I know," Elizabeth said. "That woman. That woman. She's destroyed Robert's life."

"Mom. Try to be nicer," Brenda said. But Brenda knew her mother was most likely right. Poor Sarah. She didn't need more stress with the baby on the way. Brenda would have to call her to see how she and Robert were doing.

Chapter 52

Sarah scooped out strawberry ice cream into a cup. She was busy working the lunch shift at the pharmacy. She couldn't wait for Heather to get in to help. For some reason it was busier than usual today. She wiped sweat off her brow. She couldn't wait for the baby to come. She was hot all the time and felt like all she could do was waddle. Brenda always gave her pep talks to help her feel better when she became frustrated with how difficult it was to move and sleep.

The fire at Robert's parents' place had caused additional stress. Robert and his brother had helped his parents move what they could salvage into an apartment. His mother was drinking even more now that they were displaced. Robert was more on edge than usual because of it all.

"Sarah, you okay?" Patrick, one of the town policemen, asked. He and Herb had come in for grilled cheese and milkshakes.

"Oh yes, Patrick. I'm just hot. Actually, I'm hot all the time lately. This little baby generates a lot of heat."

"Well, I bet it will be a beautiful baby, just like its mom," Patrick replied. Sarah blushed. Patrick was always so sweet to her.

"Now you made her blush, Patrick," Herb said.

"Will you two leave this pregnant woman alone." Hazel reached to take the ice cream scoop from Sarah. "Sarah, dear, you go take a short break. I can cover for a few minutes.

Everyone seems to want to be over here with you, rather than up front with me."

"Thanks, Hazel. I'll be right back." Sarah took off her apron, hung it on a peg, and headed toward the break room in the back. She passed by Richard who was on the phone. He winked as she went by. Sarah went into the break room and poured herself a glass of water. She then took the cheese and tomato sandwich she'd brought to work out of the fridge. She sat down and began eating. She was starving. The baby moved a lot as she ate. Heather rushed into the break room.

"Oh, Sarah. I'm sorry I'm late. I saw Hazel in the soda fountain. Time got away from me. I'm just distracted lately,"

"Don't worry. We're fine. Plus, you really aren't that late." Sarah took another bite of her sandwich.

"I don't know what's wrong with me." Heather began to sob quietly.

"Hey, hey. I'm the pregnant one who's supposed to be all emotional. What's the matter?" Sarah rubbed her friend's arm.

"I don't know. Teddy and Amber saw me having Chinese dinner with Richard and acted all weird. Now Dylan seems to be acting distant. Richard was just tutoring me in chemistry." Heather dried her tears with a Kleenex.

"Dylan's fine. He hasn't said a word to me about anything. He's just been busy with school and work. He's also has been really distracted by Vinny's death. Sit down, you got a few minutes?" Sarah put her hand on the chair next to her.

"Well, the other part of it is that Richard asked me if I'd have dinner with him again. It puts me in an awkward spot, especially since he works here." Heather sat down. Sarah suddenly started feeling protective towards Dylan.

"Well, what did you say when he asked you? Doesn't he know you're dating Dylan?"

"Yeah, he knows that. I actually didn't answer Richard when he asked. I just pretended like I didn't hear him, but I'm worried that he'll ask again. Then what do I do?"

"You tell him you're dating my brother. That's what you do." Sarah became annoyed; she stood up, quickly drank the rest of her water, and left the break room. She walked past Hazel and said, "I'll be right back. I just need a little air. Can I work up front at the register when I come back in?"

"Of course, dear," Hazel replied, looking back into the pharmacy area where Heather now stood next to Richard.

Chapter 53

$\mathcal{D}$ ylan was glad the semester was over because he felt mentally exhausted. Vinny's death had hit him hard. He was also annoyed because Teddy had told him that he and Amber had seen Heather with Richard at the Chinese restaurant. He'd decided not to ask Heather a lot about it. He trusted her. Dylan knew Heather struggled with chemistry and he couldn't help her since his strength was accounting and numbers.

Dylan had a week off before he started his internship at a large accounting firm in New Haven. He'd decided he would take the time to talk to a Navy recruiter. Talking to a recruiter didn't mean that he would necessarily enlist. He just wanted more information. He hadn't told a soul that he was going. He was tired of everyone giving him their opinions. Even he knew he would be better off if he waited a year until after he graduated from college.

He pulled into the parking lot of the building. There were quite a few cars there. He spotted the location of the recruiting center. He walked down and peered inside the glass front window of the office. Everything looked gray and dingy. There were older two heavyset men sitting at desks. One was talking to someone and the other was on the phone. Two young men were sitting in the waiting area. Dylan walked in. The office smelled like cigarettes and sweat.

"Welcome, young man. Please sign in. Help yourself to

coffee and have a seat. We'll be with you as soon as we can," the solider talking to the young man said.

"Thanks." Dylan poured himself a cup of coffee and then sat down in the waiting area. The other two men who were waiting nodded to him. On the table next to him was a recruitment brochure. He started skimming through it. There were all types of possible jobs listed. He came to the section of positions based in the Ship Office such as accounting, inventory, and ship supplies. He'd enjoy something like that and he'd be part of the war effort. The man on the phone hung up and called forward one of the waiting men.

"I'm Scott. Are you here to enlist?" the other man who was waiting asked Dylan.

"Just here to learn more, right now. How about you?"

"I was like you, thinking about it, but now I've decided it's time to go for it. I've always wanted to enlist. I just finished school so now it's time. My mom and girlfriend are upset with me for doing it but I explained to them I just needed to."

The recruiter then called up Scott.

"Nice talking to you," Scott said to Dylan.

"Good luck," Dylan replied. He listened to the conversations the recruiters and men were having. He could tell these men had made up their minds to join and were excited and pumped up about it. He could also tell that they were torn about leaving their families and girlfriends. He thought about Heather. He really loved her a lot. He couldn't blame Richard for being interested in her. She was beautiful and smart and hardworking. He thought about how much he loved his hometown. Suddenly he heard, "Mr. Dylan Jones."

"Yes sir. Right here sir."

"Come on up," the recruiter called.

"Hello son, I'm Chief Petty Officer Ryan James. Thanks for coming in. Have a seat." He motioned for Dylan to sit down. Dylan suddenly felt nervous; he was sweating. He shifted back and forth in the chair until he got comfortable.

"You okay?" the recruiter asked as he lit a cigarette. "Would you like one?"

"No thanks, sir. I'm here to learn more about the navy. I'm thinking of enlisting."

"Well, you got any training?"

"Yes, sir. I just finished my junior year at Quinnipiac."

"What you studying?"

"Accounting."

"You're good with numbers then?"

"Yes, sir." Dylan began to relax.

"Well, we always have a need for people who are good with numbers. We have lots of supplies and things to track on ships. Why are you interested in enlisting now? Why not wait a year and enlist after you finish school?"

"I've always been interested in the navy. My uncle was in the navy. He served on a battleship. He loved it."

"I know. I've loved the navy. You get to travel the world and learn about other cultures. Most of all you get to serve our fine country. I was in World War II."

"Thanks for your service, sir," Dylan said.

"Okay. Well, the navy is terrific. If you're interested, I got some paperwork you need to fill out." He opened the filing cabinet next to him and pulled out a folder. "Go ahead, look through it." Dylan looked through the folder.

"I need everything filled out. It asks your standard questions. Make sure to talk about your accounting background. You fill it out and return it to me and then it gets processed. It takes a few weeks. If they have an interest then they'll call you in for a physical. You got any health problems?"

"No, sir. I don't. I do have to wear reading glasses though."

"Hell, if I had to eliminate guys that wore glasses to read, I'd be short a bunch of men," the recruiter said.

"Well, I am glad you take guys who wear glasses."

"Lots of guys coming in," the recruiter whispered to Dylan. "Most want to avoid getting drafted into the army. You don't seem like that. You're in college and everything."

"Well, I just recently lost a friend in the war." Dylan looked at the floor.

"I'm sorry, son. That explains it. Well, take advice from me. I lost a lot of buddies in World War II. Don't decide anything just yet. Take a few more weeks to think about it. Maybe you should finish school then enlist. Just take your time. You seem smart, kid."

"Thanks, sir. I appreciate your time." Dylan picked up the folder, shook the recruiter's hand, and headed to the door.

Chapter 54

Sarah didn't feel well at all. Laura had driven her to the doctor's office and had asked Henry to get in touch with Robert and with Sarah's family. Sarah was worried that what she felt were contractions. It was too early for the baby to come. She tried not to panic.

She moaned in pain.

"We're almost there Sarah, hang on." Laura pressed the gas pedal down and drove even faster. Luckily Sarah's doctor was right next to the hospital.

"It's okay, Laura....ahhhhh...I'll be fine."

"Don't worry about talking. Just take care of yourself and that baby. Take deep breaths."

"What if the baby comes early? It's too soon."

"Dr. Stein knows what he's doing. All will be fine." Laura pulled into the parking lot right in front of the clinic.

"You can't park here."

"I can park here. I'm going to get you situated and then I'll move the car." Laura jumped out and went over to Sarah's side of the car and opened the door. "Come on, just hold onto me."

Laura walked Sarah up to the medical clinic.

"Come on, my dear, come back here with me." A nurse took Sarah's arm and led her towards the examining rooms.

"I'll go park the car and then I'll be right back."

Sarah's body relaxed when Laura walked into the examination room. She felt relieved to see her. Laura sat down next to Sarah and held her hand.

"The nurse said the doctor would be right here." There was a knock on the door.

"Sarah, okay to come in?"

"Of course." Dr. Stein came in, nodded at Laura, sat down, and swiveled his chair to face her. "Well, hello Sarah. What's going on?"

"A couple of hours ago I just started feeling poorly. I'm getting pains that come and go in through here." Sarah moved her hands across her stomach.

"Well, let me see what's going on." Dr. Stein put his stethoscope on Sarah's stomach. He listened intently. He then asked Sarah to move down and to put her legs in the stirrups, so he could examine her.

"Want me to leave?" Laura asked.

"No, it's fine. Please stay," Sarah said.

Sarah looked up at the ceiling and prayed that everything was okay with the baby. The doctor seemed to take a long time. "Is everything okay?"

"Well, it seems as though your little one is ready to come into the world," Dr. Stein calmly replied.

"Oh no, but it's too early," Sarah said.

"I'm sure everything will be fine. Where's your husband?"

"I believe he's on his way. Henry was calling him and Sarah's family," Laura replied as tears streamed down Sarah's face.

"Okay, can you try to get ahold of him and tell him to meet us at the hospital? You can use the phone in the receptionist area. We have time; she's just a few centimeters dilated."

"I'll be right back, Sarah." Laura hurried out.

Dr. Stein grabbed Sarah's hand. "I need you to relax.

We'll get Robert here as fast as possible. Once Laura comes back in, I'll go call the hospital and have them get ready for us. I'm going to have Laura and a nurse take you over to the admissions area and I'll meet you in Labor and Delivery."

Chapter 55

Henry had called Hazel to come in to work on her day off since Sarah had left with Laura to go to the doctor. Now that Sarah was at the hospital he was going to let Heather off early so she could go to the hospital with Dylan. Laura had sounded upset when she called Henry to tell him that Sarah's baby was coming early. Luckily it hadn't been a very busy day at the pharmacy.

Hazel came in, to cover Sarah's shift at the pharmacy. "Is Sarah okay?"

"Don't know," Heather replied. "Laura just called and said the baby is coming and that Sarah was being admitted to Milltown Hospital."

"It's a few weeks early. I sure hope the baby is okay," Hazel replied. "Let me get my smock so you can get out of here."

Heather was so worried about Sarah and she was also worried about seeing Dylan. She wondered if he was going to bring up the fact that Teddy and Amber had seen her with Richard. She'd not had a chance to discuss it with him since he'd been so busy with finals. Heather had ended up doing okay on her chemistry exam thanks to Richard. She was relieved that her classes were over for the semester.

Dylan greeted her at the door and gave her a long hug. "Thanks for coming to get me. I've missed you."

It felt good to be in Dylan's arms. She hugged him close.

"Oh Dylan. I'm so worried about Sarah and I'm sorry about having Richard help me with chemistry. There's nothing going on. Teddy and Amber looked appalled when they saw me there with him."

Dylan looked into her eyes. "Heather, we've both been stressed with end of semester things. Sure, I was a little jealous of Richard when Teddy told me but I trust you and I love you."

"I love you too."

"We better head off to the hospital. I want to be there to welcome my new niece or nephew into the world," Dylan said.

"I'm so scared for the baby. It's too early."

"Dr. Stein knows what he's doing, plus Sarah's as healthy as an ox. They'll be fine."

Laura, Elizabeth, Brenda, and Robert were in the waiting area when they arrived at the hospital. Elizabeth sat in the corner of the waiting room. She looked as white as a ghost which alarmed Heather.

"How is she?" Dylan asked.

"She's in labor. The doctor and a couple of nurses are back there with her," Robert replied.

"Can we go back and see her?" Heather asked.

"I bet you can go back and say a quick hello, just ask the nurses at the desk. They won't let Dylan back there though," Brenda said.

"I'll stay here. You go back." Dylan said. Heather walked up to the nurses' station.

"My good friend Sarah is back there in labor. Can I go back and say a quick hello?" Heather asked.

"Let me check." One of the nurses got up and went into the back. She then opened the door and motioned for Heather to come back. Sarah looked exhausted when they entered the room.

"Oh. I'm so glad you came." Tears streamed down Sarah's face. Heather saw the fear in her eyes.

"I wouldn't miss this for the world." Heather grabbed her hand and kissed her cheek.

"How on earth did you get off of work?" Sarah said.

"Henry called Hazel in. By the way, she sends her love." Heather held tightly onto Sarah's hand. "I can't wait to meet the baby."

Sarah suddenly grimaced with pain. "Another contraction, ahhhhh."

The nurse motioned for Heather to leave the room. "She'll be fine."

"I'll be right outside. Love you, my friend."

Robert's parents and Abbey and Joe had arrived. Elizabeth still sat in the corner by herself. Heather knew Elizabeth did not like Robert's mother, Mary. Elizabeth looked as though she was breathing rapidly. Heather was worried about Elizabeth because of her heart condition. Heather sat down next to Elizabeth and rubbed her hand. Brenda came up and sat on the other side of her mother. Heather figured that the best thing she could do was distract Elizabeth by making small talk. She looked at Brenda. "Brenda, when are you heading back to England?"

"I was supposed to go tomorrow, but I called Harry's family and then the airline. Luckily they said it was easy to change our tickets and postpone our flights for a couple of weeks."

"That's great, but I bet you can't wait to see Harry."

"I sure can't. This being apart for military deployments is tough. Just be thankful Dylan hasn't enlisted." Brenda looked at Dylan.

"Brenda. We're not talking about that," Dylan said.

"Not talking about what?" Heather asked.

"Ever since Vinny passed, Dylan keeps threatening to enlist in the navy."

"Dylan, you said you stopped thinking of enlisting a while ago."

"Don't worry. I'm not enlisting anytime soon." Dylan stroked Heather's arm. "You all know I just talk about joining the navy every now and then."

"You better not," Brenda said. "With what Sarah's going through now you need to be here to help her and Robert."

"I know. I know," Dylan replied. Heather suddenly felt uneasy. She started perspiring and wringing her hands. She found the whole conversation alarming. The last thing she wanted was for Dylan to go to war.

"I'm going to go outside and get some air," she said.

"I'll come with you," Dylan said.

"No need to. You stay here with your family. I'll be right back."

"Now see what you did," Heather heard Dylan say as she walked away. She closed her eyes and prayed – both that Dylan wouldn't enlist and that Sarah would be fine.

Chapter 56

renda held Sarah's hand as she screamed in pain. Elizabeth was behind Sarah with her hand on her shoulder. The doctor kept saying the baby was coming any minute. To Brenda it seemed as though the doctor had been saying that for hours. Brenda hated seeing Sarah in so much pain, her body only relaxing as she had quick rests between contractions. Elizabeth wiped Sarah's forehead with a cold washcloth as Brenda held her hand. "Sarah, I wish I could do this for you. Just keep pushing and soon it'll be over."

Sarah braced for another contraction. Brenda yelled, "Push, push, push."

Sarah grimaced in pain as she pushed.

"Here comes the baby. See the head." The doctor pointed for Elizabeth and Brenda to look.

"Oh my gosh, look at that little head." Brenda couldn't believe what she was seeing.

"Keep pushing, Sarah. It's almost over," the doctor cried. Brenda felt Sarah grab her hand forcefully as she pushed. Brenda's hand hurt but she kept it there while Elizabeth kept wiping Sarah's forehead. Brenda saw the baby come out covered in white. The doctor worked quickly with help from the nurse to clean the baby. The baby let out a tiny scream and then was quiet.

"It's a girl, it's a beautiful baby girl, look at that hair." The doctor talked as he worked.

"Oh my gosh, she is gorgeous, so little," Brenda said. Elizabeth burst into tears. Sarah lay back, exhausted.

"Can I see her?" she asked as she caught her breath. "Is she okay? Is Sophie okay?"

Brenda knew they had decided to name the baby Sophie after one of their great grandmothers. The nurse wrapped the baby in the blanket and rushed her out of the room, concern on her face. Brenda was confused. What was going on? She knew she had to focus on Sarah and helping her keep calm.

"What's wrong? Why can't I hold my baby?" Sarah panicked and sobbed uncontrollably.

"Yes, what's wrong?" Elizabeth asked. Brenda noticed the fear on her mom's face. She sternly looked at her mom, nonverbally telling her to keep quiet.

"Since she's early, we need to evaluate her and watch her carefully. She'll just be down the hall from you. I'll be back to give you an update soon. Carol is coming in to clean you up and take care of you."

A new nurse walked into the room. "Hi there, sweetie, my name is Carol. I'm here to help clean you up so we can move you down to another room."

"Mom, sit down over there," Brenda said. Elizabeth sat down, speechless. Brenda and Elizabeth sat quietly while the nurse cleaned up Sarah. Brenda tried to process everything that was happening.

"We're going to move her to a room down the hall. Can you grab her personal items while I go get someone to help me move her?"

"Sure." Elizabeth stood up and started gathering Sarah's things.

Brenda asked, "Can I go get her husband now?"

"I would wait until we get her settled in the new room. Then he can come to see her," the nurse said.

"I'll go out to the waiting room," Elizabeth said. "I'll go tell the family she is being moved."

"Are you sure, Mom?" Brenda asked.

"Yes, I'll go." Elizabeth bent and kissed the top of Sarah's head.

"Love you, Mom," Sarah said. She closed her eyes to rest as her mom left the room. Brenda knew her mom was about to ready boil over with emotion, so she was glad she left to be with the rest of the family in the waiting area. Brenda worried about Sarah and wanted to stay with her as they moved her to the new room.

Elizabeth felt like a zombie. Her body ached. She prayed her granddaughter would be okay. She walked slowly to the waiting area trying to get the confidence to tell everyone the news. She hoped the doctor would give an update soon. As she walked into the waiting area, everyone stood up and rush towards her.

"How is she?" Robert asked. Elizabeth looked at him, his face full of concern, his mother's arm around his shoulder. She felt anger rise in her throat. How she despised his mother! That fire had put so much stress on them - she wouldn't be surprised if that is what made the baby come early. She swallowed down the anger as best she could. She needed to for Robert's sake.

"Sarah's resting back there with Brenda. You have a beautiful baby girl, Robert. Congratulations." She fought back tears. Robert came over to her and enveloped her in his arms. Elizabeth held him tight for a moment.

"Hey, how's the baby?" Abbey asked, her face gray with worry.

"She's in the nursery being evaluated right now. We should know more soon."

"Is she okay? How well do babies typically do when they're this early?"

"I don't know. The doctor said he'd give us an update soon. Robert, you can go back and see Sarah once she's settled in a new room. They'll let us know."

Robert squeezed Elizabeth's shoulder. There was an awkward silence in the waiting area. Elizabeth didn't know what to do.

"Did you get to hold the baby, Mom?" Dylan asked.

"No son, they needed to take her away immediately," Elizabeth said. She saw the look of fear in Dylan's eyes.

"Elizabeth, you look exhausted. Why don't you sit down here next to me?" Abbey said. "Can I get you something to drink?"

"Actually, I want to walk. Can we go to the cafeteria?"

"Sure." Abbey took Elizabeth's arm in hers and they headed to the cafeteria. Elizabeth began weeping as soon as they left the waiting area and were headed down the hallway. Abbey said softly, "It will be okay."

Chapter 57

Sarah was fast asleep in her new room. Brenda put her finger to her lips, smiled at Robert and left so they could have privacy. The nurse had given Sarah medicine to relax her and it had kicked in. Robert thought she looked beautiful. Sarah had given him a daughter and he was thrilled, but terrified too. He wished he knew what was going on. He had seen the concern in Elizabeth's face. The doctor had not come back yet to let them know how the baby was doing. It felt like an eternity. A nurse came in to check on Sarah.

"Any word from the doctor?" Robert asked.

"He should be here soon. I know it's hard but we've had lots of deliveries today for some reason." The nurse smiled and touched Robert on the arm. Robert's mind raced with uncontrollable thoughts. He assumed the worst. He tried to think positively but he couldn't. The doctor opened the door to the room.

"Can I talk to you a second?" He motioned for Robert to follow him.

Robert followed Dr. Stein into a small office.

"Have a seat, Robert." The doctor sat down but Robert remained standing.

"Is the baby okay?" His voice cracked with emotion. He wouldn't be able to bear it if the baby had died.

"She's fine right now. But her lungs are underdeveloped. She has a 50/50 chance of surviving."

"Oh no." Robert began crying, "Is there anything you can do? There must be something."

The doctor stood up and touched Robert's arm. "I'm so sorry, Robert. She'll be cared for around the clock by a special team of nurses. We're giving her oxygen. We have to monitor her closely until her lungs develop fully. I promise you, we'll take great care of her. You can't lose hope. Who can I bring back to be with you?"

"Sarah's mom and Brenda."

"I will. Do you want me to tell Sarah when she wakes?"

"No, no. I think it's best if we do it. Can I see the baby?"

"Sure. She's in an incubator down the hall in a special room that is attached to the nursery where we'll watch her closely. She's getting IV fluids. We have her hooked up to a monitor. Do you want me to take you down there, so you know where the nursery is?"

"Yes, please. I appreciate that."

"Sure." The doctor guided Robert down the hallway. They stopped in front of a glass window. Robert saw rows of babies through the window. They were wrapped up in blankets. As he and the doctor looked through the window, the doctor said, "This is the nursery, Robert. See that door over here? Your daughter is in there. That is where premature babies get around the clock care. You can't go in there right now. You'll be able to see her and then take her home when her lungs develop."

"Can't I just go in there and see her?" Robert asked.

"No, you can't right now. We need to stabilize her. I'm sorry, Robert," Dr. Stein said.

Robert wiped tears from his eyes. He felt empty inside. "Is there anything I can do? I feel helpless. My poor daughter."

"We just have to wait, Robert. I know this is hard. We just need to be patient. Let me go get Sarah's mom and Brenda. I'll be right back." Robert sat there and sobbed inconsolably.

Chapter 58

Sarah woke up, startled, "Where's the baby?"

"She's down in the nursery," Robert said.

"I want to go see her immediately," Sarah demanded.

"You can't right now," Brenda said.

"Why? What's wrong?" Sarah asked. She looked at Robert. He wouldn't meet her eyes. She looked at her mom. Sarah's face was quivering.

"Mom, Mom, what's going on?"

Her mom came over and grabbed her hand.

"She's in an incubator because she was early. Her lungs are not as developed as they should be," Elizabeth said.

"Oh God, what does that mean?" Sarah asked. She was starting to panic. She turned towards Robert and saw the pain in his eyes. "Robert?"

"She's getting oxygen and IV fluids. They're constantly monitoring her," Robert said.

"And?" Sarah asked.

"She only has a fifty-fifty chance of living," Brenda said. Sarah couldn't believe what she was hearing. She felt as though a knife had torn through her. Her head hurt. Tears streamed down her face. She felt like she wanted to throw up.

"What?" Sarah cried. "Fifty-fifty?"

"It will be okay, Sarah. She'll be okay. We just have to wait to see if her lungs develop." Robert rubbed her arm.

"Don't touch me right now. I want to see my baby," Sarah

said. Robert took his hand off her arm. She glared at Robert with anger.

"Sarah, you have to be strong," Brenda said. "You need to heal so you can be strong for Sophie."

"I just want to see my baby. Now!" Sarah screamed. Sarah seemed out of control. Brenda ran out to get a nurse. Robert and Elizabeth just looked at one another. They were not sure what to do.

"Miss Sarah, it will be okay," the nurse said as she entered the room. "Let me give you something to relax you,"

"I want to hold my baby. I just want my baby," Sarah demanded. She kept repeating this over and over.

"I know, I know, but you can't right now," the nurse said. The nurse injected something into Sarah's IV bag. Sarah tried to protest but was asleep within seconds.

Chapter 59

Sarah was sitting up in bed, concentrating on a cross-word puzzle. The scent of flowers was overwhelming. Elizabeth smiled at the color in her daughter's cheeks. It had only been five days since Sophie's birth and Sarah looked better every day.

"Mom," Sarah said. Elizabeth kissed her daughter on top of her head.

"I got you a sky bar, thought you could do with something nice to eat for a change."

"My favorite. Thanks, Mom," Sarah said. She opened the chocolate bar and took a bite.

"Guess you were hungry," Elizabeth said.

"I've been craving chocolate. This tastes so good."

"Your dad sends his love. He's working today. Brenda is doing errands. Her trip to England is coming up soon."

"I feel bad she had to postpone it."

"Are you kidding? She was thrilled to be here when Sophie was born," Elizabeth said.

"Mom, I just want to hold Sophie," Sarah said.

"I know you do, honey. Soon. Every day that goes by is a positive sign. It means her lungs are developing and that she's getting stronger," Elizabeth said.

"I just feel terrible about everything. Eloping. The baby. Did I cause all this?"

"Of course not. Sometimes things happen and we just

can't explain why," Elizabeth said. "We just can't give up hope. I'm praying for that little girl every day."

"I am too," Sarah said.

"You want to go for a walk?"

"I would love to," Sarah said. Elizabeth helped Sarah put on her slippers. As they walked down the hall, Elizabeth held Sarah's arm. She was proud of her daughter. This was a life or death situation, but Sarah was being strong. She just hoped everything would be okay.

Chapter 60

Ten days had passed since Sarah had given birth to Sophie. She didn't want to leave the hospital, but she was being discharged today. Baby Sophie was still in an incubator. Sarah asked to go to the nursery before she left. The nurses told her that they would take her to the side room off the nursery where Sophie was, so she could see her before she left. They let her do that every day starting a few days before.

"I don't want to leave without Sophie." Dylan stopped pushing the wheelchair for a moment and rubbed his sister's shoulder.

"Don't worry, sis. Little Sophie is going to be fine. They say she's showing signs of improving each day. Don't be down."

"She'll be fine, Sarah. And we've set a schedule so someone will always be here to be with her," Heather said. Dylan knocked on the nursery door. A nurse came to get Sarah. Sarah had mixed emotions when being wheeled past the other babies in the main nursery. She thought they were beautiful and she was happy for the other moms, but she hoped her daughter would be okay.

"Here she is, Miss Sarah," the nurse said as she wheeled Sarah into the special room where Sophie was. Sarah's heart sank, as it always did. Sophie was attached to all kinds of devices. A monitor was continually beeping quietly. An IV line was running into her tiny arm. Sarah just wanted to hold her baby and tell her it would be okay. It killed Sarah that she couldn't hold her.

"Sophie, I love you sweetie. Keep strong. I love you," Sarah said as she burst into tears. The nurse handed Sarah a tissue.

"It's okay. It's okay," the nurse said as she wheeled Sarah back to the hallway.

"I just can't bear to leave her here. I'm going to go crazy."

"Now you have to toughen up, sis," Brenda said. "You have to be a fighter just like little Sophie is. Being all emotional isn't going to help Sophie. You need to go home, rest, and heal so you're ready for Sophie when she comes home. We have work to do to finish up that nursery. Now come on. I'll go pull up the car."

Robert stood staring through the nursery window.

"Come on, Robert." Dylan patted Robert on the back.

Robert shook his head. "It's just hard, Dylan. What if she doesn't make it? I haven't even been able to hold her yet."

"You'll get to hold her soon. Now come on. You have to be strong for Sarah. You have to be there for her so she can heal and get strong. We're all pulling and praying for baby Sophie." Dylan wiped a tear from his eye. "Come on, let's go. Brenda will be annoyed if she's out there with the car and you aren't there."

"That's for sure. Okay. Let's go."

Chapter 61

Elizabeth put the laundry basket on the dining room table. She'd not kept up with the laundry, she'd been at the hospital so much. Elizabeth was so worried about her granddaughter and prayed every day. She knew Sophie's chances improved with every day that went by.

Why had this happened to Robert and Sarah? They didn't deserve it. Elizabeth had always wondered about Robert's lifestyle. She'd never said a word to anyone about what she thought. No one had understood why she was so upset when Sarah eloped with Robert, but she had her reasons, and Sarah being so young wasn't the only thing she'd been worried about. Even though she loved Robert dearly, there was something else about him that bothered Elizabeth but she wasn't a hundred percent sure about her suspicions. She would confront Robert soon.

"Boy, you are deep in thought. What are you thinking about?" Elizabeth jumped at Eugene's voice.

"Oh, nothing." Elizabeth took socks out of the basket to match into pairs.

Eugene sat down in the living room and turned on the television. "Heard anything about Sophie today?"

"Not yet, but Abbey and I are going by later to check on her, want to come?" Elizabeth asked.

"Wish I could but I need to take the car in and have the

oil changed. I was going to stop at the store too, do you need anything?"

"Yes, I need some potatoes and milk. You want fried chicken for dinner?" Elizabeth placed the socks she'd matched together in a pile on the table.

"I'd enjoy fried chicken. I love your fried chicken. That's the advantage of marrying a girl who grew up in the south, she makes awesome fried chicken." Elizabeth laughed.

Elizabeth took Brenda's folded laundry and put it on her bed in her room. She picked up the photo of Harry that Brenda had next to her bed. *He sure is handsome,* Elizabeth thought. Brenda was handling being apart from him really well, but Elizabeth knew how much she missed him.

Putting Dylan's socks in his drawer, Elizabeth noticed a brochure. She picked it up and opened it. Some paperwork fell onto the floor. Elizabeth bent down to pick it up the paperwork. When she saw what it was, she called, "Eugene, Eugene."

"What's the matter?" Eugene called. Elizabeth ran down the hallway.

"Look what I found." Elizabeth pointed to the brochure. "I was putting Dylan's socks away."

"What is it? You would think something died with all your ruckus."

Elizabeth handed Eugene the paperwork. "It's an application to join the navy. He must have gone to the recruiting center. Look at this business card. Oh no, my baby boy might join the navy."

"Calm down." Eugene skimmed through the brochure. "We can't meddle in his business. He's an adult. Plus, he hasn't applied. The application form is right here."

"I don't want him to join the navy. I'd worry night and day." Elizabeth put her hand on her heart.

"Are you okay?"

"I'm okay. I just don't know what's going on. First, Sarah eloped. Then Sophie is premature and Brenda's leaving for England. Now this." Elizabeth sighed.

"Honey, our kids are growing up. They'll be fine. But I wouldn't say a word to Dylan about this. He's already worried about Sarah and baby Sophie. Go put this back where you found it. Just because he has this, it doesn't mean he'll apply. It's a positive sign that he didn't fill out the application form when he was at the recruiting center. Now go put this back."

Elizabeth reluctantly took the paperwork back upstairs and put it into Dylan's drawer. Then she grabbed her purse and car keys.

"Where are you going now?" Eugene asked.

"I'm going to pick up Abbey and then we're going to see baby Sophie." Elizabeth gave him a kiss on the forehead. "Bye, sweetie."

"Remember, you need to respect Dylan's privacy." Eugene looked into Elizabeth's eyes.

"I will. Don't worry. I'll just tell Abbey. Abbey won't tell anyone."

Elizabeth drove down Main Street towards Milltown. She turned on the radio and listened to a classical music station as she drove through town. She needed to unwind. There was so much going on in her family. Eugene was right that their children were grown up now, but that didn't mean that she didn't worry about them.

"Mom, what are you doing here?" Elizabeth heard as she walked into the bakery. She spotted Dylan at the counter talking to Joe.

"Dylan, what are you up to?" Elizabeth gave him a hug.

"Just stopped by to see Joe and Abbey. I was over at the hospital checking on baby Sophie," Dylan said.

"How is she?"

"Sarah told me they said she's getting stronger each day and her lungs are developing." Dylan took a bag of cookies from Joe.

"Thank goodness," Joe said.

"Well, Mom, see you at home later. I'm going over to Heather's to hang out." Dylan kissed his mom on the cheek. "Take care, Uncle Joe. Thanks for the cookies."

"Bye, Dylan. Abbey's in the back, Elizabeth, if you want to go find her."

"Will do."

"Elizabeth, thank goodness you're here. I need a break. Let me just finish taking these cookies off the pan." Abbey lifted a cookie off the sheet with a spatula. "Here, have a fresh-baked cookie."

Elizabeth picked up a chocolate chip cookie and took a bite. "Mmmm, Abbey, this is good."

"You've always loved warm cookies." Abbey laughed at the chocolate smeared on the side of Elizabeth's mouth. Elizabeth wiped it off with her finger.

"Dylan looked good. He sure loves that little baby. He's so excited to be an uncle."

"You know, you're right. Maybe that will keep him from going in the navy."

"He's not going to go into the navy. He's got another year of school. He's got Heather. And now he has baby Sophie." Abbey untied her apron, took it off, and hung it up.

"I hope you're right. I found some information he got from the navy and an application today." Elizabeth looked sheepishly at Abbey.

"Where did you find that?"

"In his sock drawer. I was putting laundry away." Elizabeth looked down at the floor.

"Were you snooping?"

"No, not at all. I found it by accident."

"Well then, I wouldn't discuss it. Was the application filled out?"

"No, it was totally blank."

"Well then, I wouldn't worry about it. You worry too much. Come on, let's go see your new grandbaby."

Chapter 62

Sarah felt calm when she was at the hospital with Sophie. Even though they wouldn't let her hold Sophie yet, the nurses brought Sarah in to look at her once each day and then she sat outside in the waiting area. The nurses were wonderful to her. Dylan had been there earlier; he was thrilled to be a new uncle. He'd already bought Sophie a small white teddy bear that he'd brought to the hospital with him. The teddy bear sat in the chair next to Sarah. She was going to take it home with her and put it in Sophie's nursery.

Sarah heard footsteps and looked up to see her mom and Aunt Abbey. She stood up and greeted each of them with a hug and kiss. "Thanks so much for coming."

"How's baby Sophie?" Abbey asked.

"They say she's doing well. She's growing. Getting stronger each day," Sarah said.

"She's growing. Oh my. That's great Sarah." Abbey smiled.

"I am glad she continues to keep getting stronger." Elizabeth hugged her daughter.

"I just hope it's enough. The biggest thing is her lung development," Sarah said.

"Well, she has a lot of people praying for her." Elizabeth put her hand against Sarah's. The touch of her mom's hand felt good. Sarah squeezed her mother's hand and smiled.

Dr. Stein came down the corridor towards them. "Hi there, everyone."

"Hi, Dr. Stein. Nice to see you." Sarah nervously smiled. Whenever she saw Dr. Stein she immediately started worrying what he would tell her. She could feel herself begin to sweat. Her heart began to race.

"I'm here to check on Sophie and some of the other babies. Once I'm done, I'll come find you all and give you an update." Dr. Stein went into the nursery.

"Oh, this time of day is always tough," Sarah said.

"Well, Dr. Stein seems optimistic, so we should be too," said Abbey. "Come on, let's go to the cafeteria and get something to drink. I'm parched."

"But what if he comes back out while we're gone," Sarah said.

"Come on, let him do his job, we'll be back soon enough." Abbey motioned for Elizabeth and Sarah to follow her down the hallway. Sarah paused, watching Dr. Stein in the nursery, and then followed her mother and aunt reluctantly.

"Come on, let's sit down here and eat our ice cream" Elizabeth sat down near the window in the cafeteria and patted the chair next to her. "Let's enjoy the sunshine coming in the window for a little bit."

"I'll be right back, I need to go to the restroom." Abbey said.

Sarah sat down next to her mother. She opened her ice cream and took a bite. It tasted cold and delicious. She closed her eyes and thought of when she was little. She, Dylan, and Brenda loved taking ice cream sandwich breaks when playing. She hoped her daughter Sophie would live to share that same simple joy.

"Sarah," Dr. Stein quietly said as he leant over her to get her attention.

"Yes?" Sarah opened her eyes, "Oh Dr. Stein, sorry, I was daydreaming."

"Well, I have great news. Sophie has crossed a major

milestone in her lung development. You'll be able to take her home in two days. We'll have to teach you how to care for her," Dr. Stein said.

Sarah jumped up and hugged Dr. Stein. "Oh my gosh. Does that mean I can hold her?"

"Not yet. Tomorrow. Be here at eleven o'clock with your husband."

"Thank you, doctor, thank you." Tears of happiness streamed down Sarah's face as she clasped the doctor's hands.

"What's going on?" Abbey asked, joining them. "Why are you crying?"

Chapter 63

Elizabeth was reading the newspaper in the living room while Brenda packed her suitcase. It was open on the couch. It seemed like Brenda had just been in England. It was hard to believe that several months had already passed by. Eugene and Dylan had gone fishing for the day. Elizabeth was hoping that Dylan would open up to Eugene about his plans for the future.

"I found it." Brenda held up her camera.

"Good. I loved seeing the photos you took last time. I'll look forward to seeing more," Elizabeth said.

"Mom, thanks for hanging out with me while I get ready." Brenda gave Elizabeth a hug.

"I'll miss you when you go, but I'm so glad that you have Harry."

"Oh Mom, I'll only be gone for two weeks."

"Have you figured out a wedding venue yet?" Elizabeth asked.

"Not yet. I need to have Harry back here so he can help me decide. Oops, I thought of one more thing; I need to make sure to bring my slips and nylons. I'll be right back." Brenda darted out of the living room.

Elizabeth wished that she and Eugene had money to put towards Brenda's wedding, but they didn't have much to spare with just Eugene working. Elizabeth had stopped working to raise the children and home school them. She'd decided not to return to work once they went to college be-cause she was already in her early sixties. Brenda hadn't asked if she and Eugene could help pay for her and Harry's wedding. Elizabeth didn't bring the topic up either.

Brenda came back in with a bundle of nylons and slips and placed them in the suitcase. "I can't wait to see Harry. It's been tough not seeing him in so long."

"I know. This war is keeping lots of couples apart."

"I'm glad though that I'll get to see Sarah bring Sophie home from the hospital before I leave."

"I know. Thank goodness Sophie's okay."

"Sarah would never have been the same if something had happened to Sophie." Brenda picked up the camera. "I need to take the camera to the hospital with me tomorrow so I can take photos when they leave."

"Speaking of the hospital, I probably need to get ready and head over there." Elizabeth glanced at the clock on the mantle and stood up.

"Hey, I can drive you and drop you off. I've done enough packing for today. I can do some last-minute shopping while you're at the hospital. How does that sound?"

"That would be great. It'll just take me a few minutes to get ready." Elizabeth headed toward her bedroom.

Elizabeth had felt overwhelmed with emotion for the last few days. She'd found Dylan's navy literature, she hadn't known if baby Sophie was going to survive, and Brenda was leaving to visit Harry in a few days. Elizabeth hated the idea of Brenda flying overseas. But, despite all the stress, Elizabeth's heart had remained strong. She'd not needed to go to the doctor or hospital and she was grateful for that.

Chapter 64

Robert saw Brenda dropping Elizabeth off at the front of the hospital. He had just parked the car and was walking through the hospital parking lot. He was excited that he would get to hold Sophie today. Sarah was already inside.

He hurried through the hospital entrance and looked around for Elizabeth. He spotted her going into the hospital gift shop. He followed her in. "Hi there, Mom. How are you this morning?"

"Hi, Robert. I was just stopping in to buy some Lifesavers. Can I get you anything?"

"Sure." Robert picked up a chocolate bar.

"Sure, just put it up here. You excited about holding baby Sophie today?"

"I definitely am. It's been tough."

"I know. In fact, I'd like to talk to you about that. Let's go outside in the fresh air for a few minutes."

"What's up?" Robert asked, once they were outside.

"Well. I've been thinking. This was a real close call with baby Sophie and thankfully the doctor seems to think that she'll be fine." Elizabeth fiddled with her hair. She seemed nervous to Robert.

"I know. It's such a relief."

"Robert, just be careful. That other way of life is illegal, you know. You don't want to jinx anything."

Robert looked at Elizabeth in shock. His mouth hung open.

"What do you mean?"

"You know, hanging out with men. Why do you think I didn't want Sarah to elope with you? I love you Robert, but I've noticed things. Don't hurt my daughter." Robert felt sick inside. He could feel the color draining from his face. How did Elizabeth know?

"Now don't worry. I have not and will not say a word to anyone and I will never bring it up again to you. But think about it. You chose to marry Sarah. You chose to have baby Sophie." Elizabeth stared Robert down.

Robert turned away and sat down on the wall. He was sweating profusely even though it was cool outside. He felt like he was going to throw up. If Elizabeth had noticed, then had others too? He pulled a Kleenex out of his pocket and wiped off the sweat. He didn't know what to say.

"Hey, what's wrong with you guys?" Dylan and Eugene walked over. Robert prayed Elizabeth wouldn't say anything to them.

"What are you two doing here?" Elizabeth hugged Dylan.

"We finished fishing and went to get some cookies at Abbey and Joe's." Dylan held up the bag. "Then we figured we'd stop by and see how Sophie was doing."

"Robert, you look pale. Are you okay?" Eugene asked.

"I'm fine. Just feeling a little off. If you'll excuse me a second, I'm going to head to the restroom. I'll see you all at the nursery."

Chapter 65

"Smile," Brenda said as she took a photo of Sarah holding Sophie. Sarah beamed as she held her newborn daughter. They were in the garden near the hospital entrance. The rose bushes were a perfect backdrop for the photos. The past two weeks had worn Sarah down. It had almost killed her having to leave Sophie in the hospital. She'd not been sleeping well and she felt bloated as her body recovered. She was overjoyed to be finally taking Sophie home.

"Okay, Robert, get in the photo." Brenda motioned for him to move. Robert stood behind Sarah and rubbed her shoulder as Brenda took the picture. Sarah touched his hand with her free hand. He bent down and kissed her on the cheek.

"Great shot." Brenda snapped a picture. Sarah laughed. Brenda always made her laugh.

"Now you and Dylan get in and I'll take the photos." Robert moved toward Brenda and took the camera. Brenda and Dylan moved in behind Sarah. Brenda put her arm around Dylan's waist.

"Sis, I'm going to miss you while you're in England." Dylan smiled while Robert took the photo.

"I'll miss you too. Now don't go joining the navy while I'm gone," Brenda said.

"What?" Sarah turned and looked at Dylan. "You're not going in the navy, are you?"

"No, don't worry, Sarah. I looked into it and decided to not go right now."

"You better not ever go," Sarah said.

"Brenda, now see what you caused."

"I said it on purpose because I'm serious. No going in the navy anytime soon. It's bad enough having Harry overseas. I don't need you gone too." Brenda lightly pinched Dylan's arm.

"Hey, watch that." Dylan tickled Brenda's side.

"Come on, guys. You aren't ten anymore," Sarah said.

"Alright, Sarah, we better be getting Sophie home." Robert took out his keys. "I'll go get the car."

Robert kissed Sarah on the cheek and lightly touched Sophie's face. "See you in a few minutes."

Robert walked toward the parking lot. Sarah held Sophie tighter. "Brenda, did you decide on a place for the wedding? What are you going to tell Harry?"

"I'll tell him what fun we had looking at venues, but that I need him to help me make the choice. The problem is they all cost so much."

"I know. We could always have it at our church and do the reception there too."

"That's true," Brenda said.

"Speaking of weddings, what's up with you and Heather?" Sarah asked.

"What do you mean?" Dylan said.

"The competition from Richard." Sarah eyed Dylan.

"We talked it out. Even if Richard is after Heather, she has no interest in him. But no weddings anytime soon. I really love Heather, but I need to finish school before I can even consider marriage."

"You were always the most practical one," Brenda said.

Robert pulled up with the car. Brenda opened the car door for Sarah.

"I'm going to miss you, Brenda. Mail me some postcards."

"I will and I'll bring you home a pretty new dress too." Brenda watched Sarah get into the car with Sophie. She wished she didn't have to go to England right now. She wanted to help Sarah.

"Be safe and tell Harry I said hello," Sarah said.

"I will. I'll miss you and worry about you. But Robert and Dylan promised they'd look after you while I'm gone."

"Love you."

"See you guys soon," Robert called as he pulled away.

Chapter 66

renda saw him immediately. He looked so good. Their eyes met. Brenda rushed into Harry's arms. "I'm so happy to see you," he said. "You look amazing."

His embrace was warm and welcoming. She'd missed him terribly. She hugged him tight as tears of happiness streamed down her face. "Oh, Harry. I missed you so much."

"I know. I know. It was so tough being apart but now you're here." Harry pulled back, looked at Brenda, and gave her a long, passionate kiss.

"Well, well, well. What's going on here?" Harry's dad said.

"Mom, Dad. Great to see you." Harry embraced them both at the same time. Harry's mom started crying.

"You look like you're losing weight." Harry's mom patted his stomach. "I'll need to fatten you up."

"Mom, Mom, I'm fine," Harry said. "Come on, let's go find your luggage."

When they arrived at Mrs. Singer's house, she came rushing out. "Brenda, Brenda, it's been too long."

"Hi there, Mrs. Singer." Harry waved.

"I bet you're as happy to have her back as I am," Mrs. Singer said as she ran up to Brenda and hugged her.

"I sure am." Harry kissed Brenda on the top of her head. "I'll be back in about an hour as soon as I get my parents settled at the hotel."

Brenda followed Mrs. Singer into the house. "The place smells as amazing as ever. I always love the smell of your home cooking."

"I put you in your same room. Go get settled and then come have some tea with me before Harry comes and steals you away." Mrs. Singer stopped at the bottom of the stairs as Brenda walked up toward her old room.

"I sure missed you. I'm dying for some of your tea and scones," Brenda said.

"I knew it. Coming right up." Mrs. Singer smiled as she headed into the kitchen.

Brenda hung up her dresses and put her other clothes away. She felt jetlagged but the adrenalin of being back with Harry helped. She walked downstairs and into the kitchen, where Mrs. Singer had laid out scones, cream and strawberry jam.

"Have a seat my dear. Dig right in. You must be hungry." Mrs. Singer brought a pot of tea over to the table and sat down. She poured them each a cup.

"Now, how is the wedding planning going?"

"Well, my sister and I have looked at several different venues."

"And?"

"They were all gorgeous, especially the barn, but to be honest they're all quite pricey."

"Have you talked to your parents about it?"

"Not really. The problem is my family really can't afford to pay for it and I can't either." Brenda sighed.

"Well then, why don't you get married here, on the base. People do it all the time." Mrs. Singer took a sip of tea.

"I don't know. Never thought of that. What would Harry think?"

"Are you kidding? The sooner Harry can marry you, the happier he would be." Mrs. Singer smiled.

Chapter 67

Harry carried his parents' bags into the hotel. "Come on, let's head upstairs to your room then let's get something to drink."

"Son, it's so good to be here again. I can't wait until you can come back to the United States for good." Harry's dad followed him to the elevator.

"I know, Dad, I can't wait either. I miss Connecticut a lot and I especially miss Brenda."

"She's a good girl, Harry. When are you two going to marry?" Harry's mom asked. "I thought Brenda was going to work on planning the wedding but she said she had to wait to talk with you more. Is everything okay?"

"Everything's fine. I think it just comes down to the fact that Brenda's family really can't afford to put on a big wedding and Brenda and I really don't have the money either."

"Well, no need for a big wedding. How about small and intimate?"

"I wouldn't mind that at all. I just want to be with Brenda."

"Why not just get married here. On the base?" said his dad.

"I never thought of that."

"You could do it now, while we're here. What fun that would be." Harry's mom clasped her hands.

"I don't know. I might scare Brenda off if I suggest that," Harry said.

"Think about it, son. Then you two could be together sooner." Harry's mom smiled.

"Okay, but don't say anything to her. Let me think about it. You two meet me downstairs for something to drink after you get settled."

Harry thought about what his mom had said. He'd never thought of getting married in England. He wondered how complicated it would be. He did know a guy that had done it a few months before, his friend Charlie O'Brien. He sat down in the lobby and thought for a while, then he decided to call Charlie.

"Hi, Charlie? This is Harry. You got married last year on the base? Right?"

"Hi Harry. Yes, I did. Are you thinking of getting hitched?" Charlie asked.

"I haven't talked to my fiancé yet but I'm thinking about it. How complicated is it?"

"Not complicated at all. You have to apply for a license a day ahead. You then get married at the registry office. Then you can have a ceremony at the chapel on the base if you like. I'm so glad that I did it. I could be with Diane a lot sooner."

Harry spotted his parents coming down into the hotel lobby. "Well thanks, Charlie. I have to run. My parents just got here."

"Hey, good luck man. You should get married here. Best thing I ever did. Good luck."

"You talking to Brenda?" Harry's mom asked.

"No, I called a friend who got married on the base a few months ago."

"What did he say?" Harry's dad asked.

"He said it was quite easy. You apply for a license a day ahead in town then you get married in town then you can get married in the chapel on base if you want."

"Well, that sounds positive. How exciting." Harry's mom grinned.

"Mom, you're jumping the gun." Harry kissed her on the cheek. "Enough for right now; let's get something to drink."

Chapter 68

Sophie slept quietly in her bassinet. Robert thought she looked adorable. She was tiny but she was growing bigger each day. The doctor had told them that if Sophie looked like she was turning blue that they should pinch her feet with their fingers to wake her up. It worried him quite a bit. Sarah seemed more relaxed about it. Sophie had only turned blue a few times the first couple of days she was home. They pinched her feet like the doctor said and then she was fine.

Robert gathered dirty clothes in a basket and went to the laundry room. He put a load in the washing machine, then went into the kitchen to start on dinner. He was going to make Sarah's favorite casserole. She was out shopping with Heather for new post-baby clothes.

Robert finished cutting up the vegetables and then the doorbell rang. Luckily the noise of the doorbell didn't wake Sophie up. He was shocked to see Gary at the door.

"What on earth are you doing here?" Robert looked down the stairwell to see if anyone could be listening.

"I just wanted to see if you wanted to hang out some. We haven't hung out forever."

"Get in here." Robert didn't want anyone to hear their discussion. Elizabeth confronting him about his lifestyle had really freaked Robert out. He was paranoid now that others had noticed that he hung out too much with men. Gary walked into the apartment and plopped down on the couch.

"Did I say you could sit down?" Robert glared at Gary.

"Well, I used to always sit down before you got married," Gary said.

"What do you want, Gary? I told you that I can't hang out anymore. I'm married and I have a daughter." Robert stood near the door. "Now come on, please get out of here. You're going to wake up the baby."

Gary totally ignored him. Robert felt his blood boil. He was worried that someone might find them together. Sarah had never known that he had hung out with Gary and Steve more often than she knew when she was working.

"What do you want, Gary? What if Sarah comes home?"

"You have gotten so uptight, Robert. Plenty of married men hang out with guys on the side," Gary said.

"Well, I'm not one of them," Robert said, slapping his hand against the wall. Suddenly Sophie started crying.

"Now see what you did. Gary, I need you to leave now." Robert headed to the bedroom to pick up Sophie. He rocked her. A few minutes later, he heard the front door open and close. Gary must have left. Sophie relaxed against the warmth of Robert and stopped crying. Eventually she fell asleep in his arms. He put her down.

Robert felt incredibly confused inside. He loved Sarah like no one else in the world. Yet he had this other part of him that he tried to keep in check. It was hard. He knew he wouldn't be accepted in this small town if others knew about that other side of him. That's why he'd decided to marry and have a family. Sarah provided stability for him, which he hadn't had growing up in a house with an alcoholic mother.

He wondered what had gotten into Gary. He hoped Gary wouldn't come back or cause any trouble. When he'd decided to marry Sarah, he had let that other part of his lifestyle go. He had to keep suppressing it. He took another look at Sophie, sleeping peacefully, and went back out to the living room. He gasped at the sight of Sarah, standing there glaring at Gary.

"Sarah," Robert said.

"I better be going," Gary said.

"I told Gary to wait until you came out here. What's going on here?" Sarah asked. She looked furious.

"Gary was in the neighborhood and just stopped by," Robert said.

"I'll be going," Gary said. He walked out of the door.

"I'm going to see the baby," Sarah said.

"But Sarah," Robert said.

"Don't but Sarah me - I don't want to get into right now," Sarah said. She walked into the bedroom. Robert knew that she suspected something. He could kill Gary. Why had he even showed up today?

Chapter 69

Elizabeth took the cookies from the oven. Sarah was coming over with Sophie. At the thought of her daughter, she felt the tension rise. She worried about Sarah. She hoped her discussion with Robert would help him stay focused on his life with his wife and daughter. He couldn't afford to let his other lifestyle come out or be known to others. Elizabeth had seen this type of struggle when she worked with the troubled youth at Lilac Lane. Society couldn't accept those who were 'different' and Robert could even be arrested if caught in the act.

She knew Robert and Sarah would be fine. Robert just had to let the other side of his life go for his own good and for his family. She loved Robert. She blamed a lot of his life struggles on his mother. She hadn't been a good mother to Robert or his brothers. Elizabeth heard a knock at the door and the door open.

"Sarah, is that you?"

"Sure is. It's me and Sophie," Sarah said.

"Let me hold that cute bundle of joy," Elizabeth said. She took a happy Sophie out of Sarah's arms.

"How is my sweet little grandbaby?" Elizabeth said. She gently rocked Sophie as she held her. Sophie smiled happily at her grandmother.

"The doctor said she's growing just fine. Health is perfect now."

"Thank goodness. She is so darling"

"Do I smell cookies?"

"You sure do. Chocolate chip and oatmeal raisin. Help yourself. I'll take baby Sophie into the living room with me," Elizabeth said. She thought Sarah looked stressed. She wondered what was going on. She'd wait to ask. First, she'd play with Sophie. Elizabeth had already laid out a blanket on the floor with some colorful toys and rattles that Sophie liked to look at. She put Sophie down and sat down next to her. Sarah was taking her time in the kitchen. Elizabeth heard the tea pot whistle.

"Mom, you want some tea?" Sarah asked.

"I'd love some with honey," Elizabeth said. Sophie giggled at Elizabeth. Nothing made her happier.

"What have you been up to?" Elizabeth asked.

"Well it's been hard keeping the apartment clean and caring for Sophie. Don't get me wrong, I love it. But it's exhausting," Sarah said.

"How's Robert?"

"He's fine. He's been busy too."

"How are the two of you?" Elizabeth asked.

"Fine," Sarah said. Elizabeth heard Sarah's voice crack. She knew she was lying.

"What's wrong, Sarah? I know you. Something's wrong. You look exhausted. It's more than motherhood," Elizabeth said. She shook a rattle and Sophie smiled.

"Oh, Mom. I don't want to get into it," Sarah said.

"You have to talk to someone. I'm your mom. You can tell me what's wrong. Marriage isn't easy."

"It's nothing. I just think I over-reacted to something."

"What did you over-react to? Did Robert's mother do something?"

"No, no. Not at all. It's just... Like I said, it's nothing," Sarah said.

"Is it who Robert hangs out with?" Elizabeth asked.

"Mom, what do you mean?"

"You know what I mean. Gary and Steve," Elizabeth said. She didn't look at Sarah. She figured Sarah would be more likely to open up to her that way.

"You know," Elizabeth said.

"I don't know what to think and it's not like I can talk to him about it. It's awkward."

"What happened?" Elizabeth asked.

"I came home from work one day and Gary was at the apartment," Sarah said. "I didn't say anything and I still haven't said anything. I find his relationship with Gary unusual. You know what they say about Gary."

"It's probably best not to say anything to him. I think Robert has made his choice and that choice is you. He loves you. He loves Sophie. He's a terrific father."

"I know. It's just awkward," Sarah said.

"Just focus on your life with Robert and Sophie. Don't bring up your doubts or worries to him about that stuff. There is not much you could do anyway. You're married. You have a child. He'll be faithful. Have you seen Gary around a lot?"

"No, that was the only time since we've been married he's been over."

"Well, maybe Gary was there uninvited," Elizabeth said.

"I'm just confused and tired. I miss Brenda too."

"I know you do. You'll be fine. It's tough when you're first married with a young child. I'm proud of you Sarah. You've done a great job being strong. You had to deal with her coming early and not knowing if she'd make it. You've been doing a great job raising her while working part-time. Don't be too tough on yourself. Look at this gorgeous little thing." Elizabeth smiled at Sophie.

"I guess you're right," Sarah said.

"And talk to me anytime. I love you, Sarah," Elizabeth said.

"I love you too, Mom."

Chapter 70

$\mathcal{B}$ renda heard a knock on Mrs. Singer's front door. She hoped it was Harry. She longed to be with him.

"It's just me." Harry came into the kitchen with a big grin on his face.

"Come on in, Harry, sit down and have a quick cup of tea and a scone."

"How could I pass that up? Don't get up, just tell me where the cups are."

"Right there. And get yourself a plate too."

Harry took a tea cup and small plate down from the cupboard and placed them on the table. He sat down and leaned over and gave Brenda a kiss. Mrs. Singer poured him tea and put a scone on his plate. "We've been sitting here planning your future."

"You have, have you?"

"Yes, we have. I think you two should get married on the base," Mrs. Singer said. Brenda blushed. She couldn't believe Mrs. Singer had just said it out in the open. Brenda hadn't even had time to process the idea yet.

Harry choked on his tea. He composed himself and laughed.

"I can't believe you just said that. Are you in cahoots with my parents? They just suggested the same thing."

"Well, that settles it then." Mrs. Singer stood up. "It's meant to be. We need to plan a wedding!"

"We haven't even had time to discuss it though." Brenda nervously looked at Harry for guidance.

Harry grabbed Brenda's hand. "What do you think, sweetie? We were going to get married anyway. This way we could then live together sooner."

"Well, I haven't had a chance to think it through, plus I think I'm jetlagged. Can I sleep on it?"

"Of course you can. If we decide to get married here, then we need to get a license and get married at the registry office. Then we can have a wedding at the chapel."

"How do you know all that?"

"I called my friend Charlie who got married on base a few months ago. He told me everything we would have to do."

"Oh, this will be wonderful. We could have the shower here in a few days. I could take Brenda and your mom shopping in town for dresses." Mrs. Singer couldn't contain her excitement. Brenda's heart was racing. This was all happening so fast.

"We could have the reception at the mess hall." Harry smiled. "Yeah, come to think of it, I've been to wedding receptions there. They had awesome food."

"You have a major sweet tooth, Harry," Brenda said.

"There's no denying that." Harry stood up. "We better get going. Thanks, Mrs. Singer, for the tea and scones. We'll keep you posted on what we decide, and thanks for offering to help."

"I'd love to help with this. A wedding would be a great distraction from all the wartime stuff going on. Plus, you two belong together."

"Thanks for all this." Brenda hugged Mrs. Singer. "I missed you a lot and I'm so glad that I can stay with you again."

"Me too. Now you two run along and let me straighten

this place up." Outside, Brenda saw a red MG with its black top down sitting in the driveway. Harry walked over to it.

"Nice car. Who's is it?" Brenda asked.

"Mine, now hop in." Harry got into the driver's seat.

"When did you get this nice car?" Brenda got into the passenger side and put on her seatbelt.

"A couple of weeks ago. I wanted to surprise you. You better hold on. This car can move."

Harry pulled out of the driveway and sped up the road. The weather was gorgeous. There wasn't a cloud in the light blue sky. Brenda grabbed the side of the door and braced herself as Harry sped along. Then she relaxed as she got used to Harry's fast driving and being in a convertible. Brenda giggled and Harry smiled. Brenda loved the feeling of the wind in her hair. Harry drove into Huntingdon and parked near the river.

"Come on, I brought a blanket, and some wine and cheese." Harry got out of the car and opened the small trunk.

"Wow, you even have a picnic basket. I'm impressed."

"Anything for my girl." Harry handed Brenda the blanket and then he grabbed the picnic basket. He shut the trunk and took Brenda's hand. Her heart raced.

"Do we need to put the top up?" Brenda asked.

"No, it should be fine. Plus, I'm just taking you down to that grassy knoll." Harry pointed, "We'll be able to see the car from there."

They walked hand in hand along the river. Brenda felt on top of the world. She was nervous though, about how Harry was reacting to all of this talk of marrying now, rather than waiting and getting married in Connecticut. She also had her doubts as to what they should do. She just wanted to forget all that right now and enjoy the afternoon. Harry stopped at the grassy knoll and put down the picnic basket. He spread out the blanket. He sat on the blanket and grabbed Brenda and pulled her down on top of him. She laughed as he began to kiss her. She felt limp in his arms as his hands moved over her body.

"Wow, you feel amazing." Harry caressed Brenda's arm as he looked into her eyes.

"So do you. I have so been longing for this." Brenda kissed Harry passionately again. A young family walked past them. Harry pulled back a little and waved as they passed.

"If we go any further, we'd need a room," Harry said. "Let's check out what's in the basket."

There were grapes, cheese, crackers, a small bottle of wine, a corkscrew, a tiny cutting board, chocolate truffles, wine glasses, small plates, knives, and light blue napkins. Harry took the bottle of wine and uncorked it carefully. Brenda held the glasses up as Harry poured them each some wine. "To my beautiful future wife. You have made all my dreams come true and I can't wait until we start our life together permanently."

Brenda clinked her glass against Harry's. "I can't wait either."

"So, do you think we should get married now?"

"I really don't know."

"I actually think it's a great idea. If we get married then I can put in for family housing. You could go home and settle everything and then come back and live with me here."

"Well, it would be easier than planning a wedding in Connecticut right now since it's tough for you to come home. My parents really can't afford to throw me a wedding anyway and I would feel guilty if I asked for one." Brenda took another sip of her wine. "But I don't want us to rush into anything. Plus, Sarah would kill me if I got married without her being there."

"Why should she care? She eloped and you couldn't go to her wedding," Harry said.

Chapter 71

Harry couldn't believe he was getting married in two days. He was thrilled. Ever since Brenda had arrived in England, everything had happened at a whirlwind pace. He couldn't believe he hadn't thought of them getting married on the base, but when his parents and Mrs. Singer had separately come up with the idea, he knew it was right. He loved Brenda with all his heart and couldn't wait to be with her all the time.

Harry grabbed his keys and headed down to his car. He put the top down. He was going to pick up his dad, who loved riding in the MG. His mom had already gone over to Mrs. Singer's to help cook and prepare for the shower. His dad was out in front of the hotel waiting.

"Hey, Dad," Harry called as he pulled up.

"Hi son." Harry's dad opened the door and got in. "You look happy."

"I am, Dad. I'm glad you and Mom are here for the shower and wedding. It's neat how it all worked out."

"I'm so proud of you, Harry. First the air force and now marrying a good woman like Brenda. I'm really happy for you both."

"You know I have to thank Eva Marie. She was the connection that brought Brenda and me together. I wish she could be here for the shower."

"Oh, don't you worry. Your mom's already talked to the

family and they plan to throw a huge celebration next time you and Brenda are both back in Connecticut."

"I know. I bet Brenda's family will want to do something too."

"Well, they should combine forces. It's a shame they can't be here."

"I know, but it actually seemed to take the pressure off of Brenda. She knew it would be a stretch for her family to throw a wedding." As they walked into Mrs. Singer's house, they could smell Italian food.

"Smells like your mother's cooking," Harry's dad said.

"Here's the groom now." Mrs. Singer kissed Harry on the cheek and then shook Harry's dad's hand.

Harry's mom was stirring a pot on the stove and Brenda was standing and talking with some of Harry's friends. Harry kissed his mom on the cheek and then he walked up to Brenda and grabbed her from behind. She squealed with delight and turned and kissed him.

"Hey, you two need to wait until the honeymoon," Harry's friend Charlie teased.

"Wow, it's great that everyone could come," Harry said. It touched him that everyone had come to celebrate. Mrs. Singer and his mom were placing lasagna, spaghetti and meatballs, garlic bread, a cut up roast, mashed potatoes, and green beans on the table. The table was set up buffet style. There was also a decorated cake with vanilla frosting and blue trim that read *Congratulations Harry and Brenda* in blue with two gold wedding rings linked together.

"Come on everyone, help yourself to food," Mrs. Singer called.

"Before you do, I'd just like to thank everyone for coming. And I want to thank Brenda for being crazy enough to marry me on such short notice. I also think we all need to thank Mrs. Singer; not only does she open her house and welcome in our girls from back home, but she also is an amazingly generous person who welcomes us all into her life. Here's to Mrs. Singer."

"To Mrs. Singer." Everyone raised their glasses. Mrs. Singer blushed.

Chapter 72

*H*eather opened the oven door with one hand and grabbed the casserole dish. The lasagna looked perfect. Dylan stood next to her with a corkscrew in his hand. He was about to open a bottle of red wine. Robert tossed a salad near the sink while Sarah looked on as she fed Sophie a bottle.

"Wow, Heather, the lasagna smells delicious," Sarah said. Heather thought Sarah looked stressed. She wondered what was going on. It was probably just adjusting to the new baby. Sarah also had said Robert was on edge because of the fire at his parents' house. This was probably impacting Sarah too. Heather had heard sometimes women got depressed after having babies. But Sarah had wanted to be a mom more than anything else.

"Yeah, thanks so much to both of you for bringing dinner."

"It was just an excuse to see Sophie," Dylan said. They all laughed. Sarah put the bottle down and held up Sophie next to her shoulder to burp her.

"Alright, I think we're ready to eat." Heather brought the lasagna over to the table.

"Perfect timing, Sophie's asleep." Sarah took the baby into the bedroom.

"Let's all sit down." Robert sat down first. Heather and Dylan followed.

"Wine?" Dylan asked as he held up the bottle. Heather and Robert nodded yes. "Thanks again guys for doing this," Sarah said. "I love seeing you guys."

"Alright, everyone, let's have a toast. To baby Sophie. She's made me an uncle and I love it." Dylan held up his glass. The four of them clinked their glasses together. Heather enjoyed watching how much Dylan enjoyed Sophie. She thought he'd make a great father.

"Let me serve this." Heather cut the lasagna and gave everyone a piece. Robert passed the salad around while she did.

"You'll make someone a great wife one day." Sarah winked at Heather. Heather saw Dylan shift in his chair.

The phone rang. Sarah jumped up to get it so it wouldn't wake up Sophie. "Hello, oh, hi Brenda. Where are you?" There was a pause.

"You what?" Sarah asked.

"What's wrong?" Dylan asked.

"Well, congratulations, sis. Yes, I will tell everyone. Did you tell Mom yet?"

"Tell Mom what?" Dylan asked.

"No way. Okay, I'll let you go. Love you, Brenda." Sarah hung up the phone.

"Well?" Robert said.

"Brenda's getting married tomorrow."

"No frigging way." Dylan slapped the table.

"Yes, she's getting married at the registry office and then at the church chapel on the base."

"Did she tell your mother?" Heather asked.

"She sure did and I guess my mom took it well."

"That's incredible," Robert said.

"Well, guess we need another toast, to Brenda and Harry. May they have a wonderful, happy marriage." Sarah held up her glass.

"Hear, hear." Dylan raised his glass. Heather and Robert held up their glasses too.

"Guess that just leaves you, brother." Sarah looked straight at Heather who blushed.

Chapter 73

$\mathcal{B}$ renda woke up to the aroma of coffee. She couldn't believe that today was the day that she was getting married. She had never been more sure of anything in her life. She loved Harry dearly and couldn't wait to be able to be with him always. She just wished Sarah, Dylan, Eva Marie, and her parents could be there, but by marrying Harry now, she wouldn't have to be apart from him long term anymore. All she had to do was go home, resign from her job, take care of things, and move to England. Once they were officially married, Harry could apply for married housing.

"Rise and shine." Mrs. Singer appeared at the door carrying a tray with coffee and freshly-baked coffee cake. "Just making sure you're awake."

"Come on in." Mrs. Singer brought over the tray and put in on Brenda's lap.

"Thank you so much. You didn't need to do this," Brenda said.

"I wanted to. This is one of the most important days of your life. I still remember my wedding day. It's one of my treasured memories. I also want to give you this." Mrs. Singer pulled out a small blue box from her pocket.

Brenda opened it. "Oh my gosh. It's gorgeous." Brenda pulled out a gold necklace which had a light blue flower pendant on it.

"Something old, something borrowed, and something

blue." Mrs. Singer smiled at Brenda. "I wore that necklace on my wedding day and I would like for you to have it."

"I can't, Mrs. Singer."

"Please take it. I see the immense love that you and Harry have for one another and I'd like you to have it. And when you have a daughter and she gets married, please pass it on to her. I have had a wonderful marriage and I think it's time to pass it on." Mrs. Singer stood up, leaned over, and hugged Brenda.

"Thank you so much." Tears of happiness streamed down Brenda's face.

"Now go ahead and eat and drink your coffee. Notice I made you coffee instead of tea because I know how much you love coffee."

"I noticed. After I eat, I'll get ready and be down." Brenda gently put the necklace back in the box and put it on the nightstand. She then grabbed the coffee mug and took a big sip. Mrs. Singer went back downstairs. Brenda finished breakfast and got ready. It was almost nine; Harry would be here in five minutes. Perfect timing.

Brenda opened her dresser drawer and took out the black box out which contained the wedding ring she'd bought Harry. She put the box in her purse and headed downstairs.

"You look fabulous." Mrs. Singer eyed Brenda's outfit. "Smart-looking suit. Good choice."

There was a knock at the door. "That must be Harry."

Mrs. Singer opened the door. Brenda saw Harry standing there in a black suit with a white shirt and a black tie. He held a bouquet of red roses.

"Come on in, Harry. You two sure make a good-looking couple."

"Thanks, Mrs. Singer." Harry stopped suddenly inside the doorway when he spotted Brenda. "You look amazing. These are for you,"

"So do you." Brenda kissed Harry and took the roses from him.

"Where are your parents, Harry?" Mrs. Singer asked.

"My friend Charlie is driving them to the registry office. We'll meet them there."

"I'm thrilled for you two. I'm going to finish making the cake while you're gone. I'll either be here when you get back or at the mess hall setting up the cake." Mrs. Singer gave them each a hug.

Brenda and Harry walked out the front door and to his MG. "You make me so happy, Brenda. I'm so honored that you're going to marry me."

"I love you so much, Harry." Brenda embraced Harry before she got into the car. "This is the happiest day of my life."

Harry and Brenda returned to Mrs. Singer's house about two hours later. She ran out the door to greet them. "How did it go? You're both beaming. Let me see the rings."

Brenda and Harry held out their hands.

"Gorgeous. Congratulations, Mr. and Mrs. Rigoni."

"I can't believe I'm Mrs. Rigoni," Brenda said.

"Well, come on in. I have a little surprise for you."

On the table was a large three-tier wedding cake with a bride and groom on the top with red roses on each level of the cake. Next to it was a matching small wedding cake decorated with a bride and a groom on top and red roses. Brenda couldn't believe how fabulous the cakes looked.

"I made this little cake so we could celebrate a little now. I also have a bottle of champagne." Mrs. Singer picked up the bottle. "Harry, will you do the honors?"

"Sure thing." Harry took the bottle from Mrs. Singer. He struggled a little as he opened it, but then the cork flew off.

Mrs. Singer set down three crystal glasses. Harry poured them each a glass and handed it out.

"To Harry and Brenda. May God bless your marriage."

"Now you need to cut your cake." Mrs. Singer handed Brenda a cake cutter. Brenda put down her glass and cut a piece of cake for each of them.

"This cake is wonderful. Oh, it's so good." Harry savored every bite. "Mind if I have another piece before I take off to get ready for the wedding at the chapel?"

Brenda laughed. Harry seemed so happy. Mrs. Singer cut Harry another piece of cake and put it on his plate. "Have as many pieces as you like."

Harry gave Brenda another kiss in between bites of cake. She couldn't believe that tonight she would share a bed with him. She couldn't wait. Harry's parents had booked a room for them at the hotel in town. His parents also had got them two nights in a hotel in Saint Andrews, Scotland as a wedding present. They were going to leave the next morning.

Chapter 74

After having cake with Brenda and Mrs. Singer, Harry headed back to his barracks so he could rest a little. He had taken the wedding ring from Brenda so that they could use it in the ceremony at the base chapel. Brenda was going to rest too and then get into her wedding dress. Harry was also going to change into his uniform. As he drove toward his barracks, he felt really happy that he had Brenda to share his life with.

Harry went into his room and took off his suit. He held out his hand and stared at his wedding ring. He couldn't believe he was married. He smiled and then closed his eyes. He thought about how he would have to take off the ring so that Brenda could put it back on him at the chapel ceremony. Then he fell asleep.

Harry woke to the sound of his alarm. Then he got up and put on his uniform. He took his ring off and put it in the box it had come in. He put the box with the ring in his pocket. He had to meet the bakery delivery man at the mess hall. He strode across the grass quad and went into the mess hall. It was quiet. There were a couple people working. He saw the tables set up in the back for them. There was a buffet table and a cake table. Both of the tables had red tablecloths on them. Mrs. Singer's amazing three-tier cake sat in the middle of a table with red rose petals surrounding the base of the cake. Then there were tables for the guests that had white tablecloths on top with red roses sitting in clear vases. It all looked gorgeous.

Harry sat down on the stone wall outside of the mess hall and bowed his head in prayer. He was thankful for the beautiful day and for God answering his prayers by bringing Brenda into his life. Suddenly a small van pulled up. It was the baker. "Sorry, I'm running a little late."

"No problem, you're hardly late at all." Harry walked toward the back of the van. The baker opened the back doors of the van.

"Can you grab one of those platters of sandwiches?" the baker asked Harry.

"Of course." Harry lifted a sandwich platter out of the back of the van. The platter contained tuna fish rolls. There were other platters of small sandwiches with cold cuts. There were also bowls of salads - green salad, fruit salad, and pasta salad. Behind all of this there were platters of cookies and little cakes. His mom and dad had ordered the food. It looked delicious. Harry and the baker made a few trips back and forth to and from the van. Soon food covered the buffet table. The baker even had red napkins, plates, and disposable silverware. The mess hall agreed to provide the hot and cold drinks. They even had agreed to provide someone who would get people drinks. His mom had thought of everything. He appreciated it.

Harry walked the baker out to the van. "Thanks for everything."

"Congratulations." The baker got into his van. "I hope you and your wife will be as happy as my wife and I are."

Harry waved to the man as he drove away. He then walked over towards the chapel. As he walked, he saw his mom and dad standing in the lawn talking to his friends. Everyone was dressed up. They all surrounded Harry to wish him well. Harry was a little overwhelmed. It warmed his heart that all these people had come to celebrate with him and Brenda.

"Come on, Harry. Let's get up to the front of the church before Brenda arrives." His friend George patted Harry on the back. Harry and his dad followed George to the front of the church. Harry walked over to the minister and shook his hand.

"Thanks for doing this for us."

"It's my pleasure, Harry. Do you have the rings?"

"Sure do." Harry pulled the ring boxes from his pocket and handed them to George. Harry watched as more guests came into the chapel and sat down. The organist started playing. Harry spotted Brenda at the back of the chapel with Mrs. Singer at her side. The sight of Brenda took his breath away. Her gown was floor-length with lots of lace and her veil flowed to the floor. The veil lightly covered her face. Brenda held a bouquet of red roses with baby's breath spread throughout it. Brenda started slowly walking down the aisle with Mrs. Singer. Harry's friend Alan was in the aisle taking photos of Brenda as she approached them. Harry was overwhelmed with joy.

When Brenda got to Harry, Mrs. Singer raised the veil up over Brenda's head and to the back and then stood to the side. Brenda smiled at Harry. A tear fell down Harry's face. The minister started the service. As the service went on, Harry gazed at Brenda and smiled. When it got to the part with the rings, Harry's dad handed him the ring that he then put on Brenda's finger when he said his vows. Mrs. Singer handed Brenda the ring that she put onto Harry's finger when she said her vows. The minister then said, "You may kiss your bride."

Everyone clapped and cheered as Harry gave Brenda a long passionate kiss.

Chapter 75

Sarah washed coffee mugs at the soda fountain. She had an early shift because she had to take Sophie in for a check-up with Dr. Stein. Gus walked in the front door. "Good morning everybody."

"Hi there, Gus," Sarah called as Gus walked over to Hazel who was folding papers at the front counter.

"Here's your paper," Hazel said.

"Thanks, Hazel. Hey Sarah, can I get a coffee to go too?"

"Coffee? You hardly ever get coffee. What's the matter? Late night?" Hazel went back to folding papers.

"As a matter of fact, yes. My wife decided to have a bunch of friends over last night to play cards. Man, did they make a lot of noise."

"Two sugars, right Gus?" Sarah asked.

"You got it. Hey, how is your little one doing?" Gus sat on one of the stools at the soda fountain.

"She's doing great. Growing quite a bit." Sophie was doing great but she and Robert were not. Robert was still stressed because of the fire at his parents' house. His mom had become more unbearable because she was living in an apartment. Luckily, she hadn't visited much since the baby had come. Robert's dad visited more. Sarah was still angry that Robert was hanging out with Gary. She didn't know what it meant, but there wasn't much she could do. She was married now with a baby. She had to make her marriage work, because there weren't many other options. Eloping hadn't been what she'd thought it would be. She had to focus all her energy and thoughts on Sophie. She wouldn't even discuss her suspicions with Robert.

"I'm so glad. I was worried with everything you had to go through. I'm glad it worked out. Got any photos?"

"As a matter of fact, I do." Sarah pulled a photo out that she had below the counter and showed Gus.

"She sure is cute, Sarah. How's Brenda? I heard she was visiting Harry in England."

"Well. Turns out she's marrying Harry while she's over there."

"What?" Hazel said.

"No way," Gus said.

"Yes, it's true." Sarah began to dry off and put away the mugs she'd washed.

"Is she coming back at all then?" Hazel asked.

"Well, she'll come back but then she will eventually go over to England and live with Harry," Sarah replied. "I'm happy for her but I'll miss her terribly."

"Oh man. How is your mom going to react?" Hazel asked.

"She already knows and is fine with it."

"I bet she's happily distracted by baby Sophie," Gus said.

"She sure is. She comes over whenever she can. She's a huge help."

"Well, we need to throw a party for Brenda before she moves to England." Hazel picked up the phone. She started dialing.

"Who are you calling?" Sarah asked.

"Eva Marie." Hazel held the phone to her ear. "Hello, Eva Marie, this is Hazel down at the pharmacy. I'm good. Hey, did you hear the news about Brenda? You have? Any ideas on what type of party we should throw for her? Hmmm." Hazel looked up toward the ceiling while she listened to Eva

Marie on the phone. After a few minutes Hazel said, "Great idea. Come on down at lunch and we can discuss it more."

"Well, what did she say?" Sarah asked.

"Her family wants to throw Brenda a big party. They have some relative with an Italian restaurant in Milltown. Eva Marie's family is ecstatic. She's coming down on her lunch break." Hazel smiled. "I love romance. Who would think we would have all this love and romance at a soda fountain?"

They all laughed. "Well ladies, I need to get on to work." Gus picked up his coffee and paper.

"You have a great day, Gus."

"Hi there, Sarah." Eva Marie placed her purse on the counter as she sat down.

"Don't you look nice? Is it a special occasion?" Sarah asked.

"Going to see a show in New Haven tonight with Walter," Eva Marie replied.

"What can I get you to drink?" Sarah asked.

"I'll take a Coke and then can I get a grilled cheese? I'm starving." Eva Marie rubbed her stomach.

"Sure thing. What do you think about that crazy sister of mine?"

"I think the fact they're getting married is fantastic. Now she'll be my cousin. I'm so happy for the two of them. My family is already going crazy with planning a party for them. As soon as Harry called to tell us the news, it spread like wildfire across the whole extended family. Everyone's always loved Harry and they worried about him being alone and in the war. Now he'll have Brenda with him by his side all the time."

"I'm excited too. I just wish I could have been over there to see the wedding."

"Me too." Eva Marie took another sip of Coke. "Can I get another one? I'm thirstier than I thought."

Sarah nodded yes. Three high school students came in. She knew them from her church. "The usual, guys?"

They nodded and started talking amongst themselves. They ordered hot dogs and chocolate shakes every day that they came in. Sarah flipped over Eva Marie's grilled cheese. "Wonder where Heather is? She was supposed to be here ten minutes ago."

Heather suddenly burst through the front door of the pharmacy and headed toward the soda fountain. "Sorry I'm late. Let me just put my stuff in the back and I'll be right back up."

Sarah brought over Eva Marie's sandwich. "So, what's your family planning?"

"They want to throw a surprise dinner for Brenda at one of my cousin's restaurants in Milltown. They want to have our extended family come, your whole family come, and Brenda's friends. You know they'll cook amazing Italian food and have great wine."

"What can I do?" Heather asked.

"Can you make them their chocolate shakes? I can start their hot dogs on the grill." Sarah turned back to Eva Marie. "Can you ask your family what we can do for the party?"

"You don't really have to do anything."

"How about we do the cake and some cookies? I can get my aunt and uncle to make everything."

"Well, they do make awesome cakes. Okay, let me check with my mom."

"And we can do the flowers for the tables. My mom loves to put together flower arrangements."

"I'd like to do something for the party too." Heather

was mixing up the milkshakes one by one on the machine. "Sarah, I'm so sorry for being late. I had to stop by the community college to register to take classes in the fall and the lines were longer than I expected."

"Don't worry about it. Was Henry okay with it? He's been quietly back in the pharmacy all day. Working on something."

"Yeah, Henry was fine with it. He's working on an advertisement."

"An advertisement for what?"

"An advertisement for a new pharmacist. Richard called him this morning to give his notice. That's probably why Henry's quiet. He just told me he's pretty frustrated. It's hard to keep a pharmacist. I can't believe Richard is leaving already."

"Where's Richard going?" Sarah asked.

"Into the army. Turns out there's a shortage of pharmacists," Heather replied. Sarah gulped. Well, at least Dylan's competition was leaving town.

Chapter 76

Harry sped through the green valleys and mountains of northern England. Last night had been unbelievable. Making love to Brenda was even better than he'd imagined. Brenda smiled at him as they passed sheep grazing in the dark green fields.

"This is so lush and green," Brenda said. "They were sure right about leaving with a full tank of gas. There's nothing out here."

"I know. That's what makes it so breathtaking. We're almost to the border. We'll stop there and take photos." Harry lightly touched Brenda's hand. They drove another fifteen minutes and then Harry pulled over at a rest area. There were a few tourists taking their photo at the border sign.

"I have the camera." Brenda pulled the camera out of her handbag.

"Great, let's go take some photos." Harry leaned in and kissed Brenda. She kissed him back hard then opened her door and got out. They walked up the path to the sign and waited until others were done taking photos.

"Do you mind taking our photo?" Brenda asked a young couple.

"Not at all." Brenda and Harry posed while the woman took their photo.

"Thanks so much," Brenda said as the woman handed

her their camera back. She and Harry then walked hand in hand down a path through the fields.

"Feels good to stretch," Brenda said.

"Sure does." Harry stopped and pulled Brenda toward him. He embraced her and kissed her passionately.

"Wow." Brenda pulled back a little and looked at Harry. "We better stop before I lose control."

"Well then, let's get up to Saint Andrews." Harry grabbed her hand and pulled her in the direction of the car park. Brenda started running toward the car. Harry ran to catch up to her. He caught up to her near the car and grabbed her around the waist. She laughed and turned toward him. He kissed her again. When he stopped he gazed into her eyes.

"Come on. You better get me to our guest house."

"What a cute town," Brenda said as they drove into Saint Andrews. Harry watched her take in all the sights. The guest house was made of gray stone and had black shutters and a thatched roof. There were beautiful gardens surrounding it. In the back yard was a small cottage. Flowers lined the window boxes of the cottage. Harry knew that was what his parents had rented for them. He hadn't told Brenda yet that they had their own cottage.

Harry pulled into the car park in front of the main house. "We're here."

"Can't wait to see our room. This place is beautiful." A pleasant-looking middle-aged woman with short gray hair came to the door.

"You must be Harry and Brenda. Welcome, welcome. Come on in. I'm Mrs. McGregor." Harry and Brenda walked into the guest house. The foyer and front room were perfectly decorated with antique furniture.

"Congratulations. Your dad said you just got married."
Mrs. McGregor fumbled through a basket. "Let me find
your key and I'll take you back to the cottage and show you
around."

"Cottage?" Brenda was grinning.

"Yes, you're in the honeymoon cottage. Found it." Mrs.
McGregor took a key out of the basket. "Come on, I'll take
you over there."

Harry and Brenda followed Mrs. McGregor into the
kitchen and out of the back door of the guest house and
over to the cottage. Beautiful gardens with bird baths and
feeders lined the pathway.

"Breakfast is eight to ten in the main house. I serve a traditional Scottish breakfast." Mrs. McGregor walked up the
front steps of the cottage and opened the door. "Go on in."

Harry followed Brenda through the door. The place was
picturesque. In the living room was a large brown leather
couch with a glass coffee table in front of it. On the table
was a clear vase filled with red roses. Next to it was a bottle
of champagne sitting on ice and two crystal glasses. A tray
of petite dessert cakes sat next to the champagne along with
about a dozen chocolate truffles.

"Wow, this is so amazing," Brenda said. "Thank you so
much."

"Let me show you the kitchen." Mrs. McGregor moved
across the living room into the small kitchen area. In the
kitchen there was a white table and two white chairs. On the
table was a small vase filled with white carnations.

"The kitchen has everything you need. I also stocked
it with coffee, tea, honey, orange juice, milk, and sugar in
case you want to make something to drink." Mrs. McGregor
opened the refrigerator to show Brenda and Harry what was
is in it. "In the afternoon I always put out a dessert with

hot tea around four in the main house. Come by if you can. Today I made apple cake. I'll leave you both alone."

"Mrs. McGregor. This is all so perfect. I can't thank you enough." Harry shook Mrs. McGregor's hand.

"It's my pleasure. I enjoy opening up our place to others. Now remember it's a short walk to the beach in case you want to see the amazing view. Just get on the road and head to the right and you'll eventually see a path on the right. Bye for now." Mrs. McGregor walked out the front door and closed it behind her.

Brenda walked over to Harry and looked him in the eyes. "Harry. This is heavenly. Should we head into the bedroom now or later?"

"Now." Harry's heart raced as he grabbed Brenda's arm and led her into the bedroom.

The past couple of days had been totally amazing, and Harry was sad that the honeymoon was almost over. He and Brenda had taken long walks on the beach and along the famous Saint Andrews' golf course. The scenery was gorgeous. They had enjoyed romantic dinners by candlelight in town. They had taken the train to Edinburgh for the day to see the famous castle. He couldn't bear the thought of Brenda returning to Connecticut for a few weeks.

"What are you thinking about?" Brenda sat down next to him on the blanket. He broke out of his trance.

"Just missing you already," Harry said. He leaned in and kissed her.

"No point in missing me yet. I'm here in the flesh and blood," Brenda said. "Come on, let's go back to the cottage and I'll make you dinner. I can do my wifely duties before I leave. We can stop at the store on the way back."

"Okay, okay. I know you're just trying to distract me. That's what I love about you." Harry kissed Brenda and then stood up. He grabbed Brenda's hand to help her up. They picked up the blanket and shook out the sand before they folded it up. Harry thought about how beautiful she looked.

"Come on. You're getting that sad puppy dog look again." Brenda grabbed his arm. They walked down the road arm in arm.

"You're amazing, Brenda. You sure read me like a book." Harry kissed her on the cheek.

"It's not hard." She smiled at him. "Oh, look over there. What a cute dog."

Harry looked over and saw a black Scottish terrier being walked by an older woman. The dog had a red collar and leash. Suddenly he felt Brenda let go of his arm. She looked both ways and went racing across the street up to the woman and the dog. He saw Brenda speak to the woman and then she started petting the dog. Harry checked to make sure no cars were coming and then he joined Brenda across the street.

"Isn't he adorable, Harry?" Brenda continued to pet the dog, which was wildly wagging his tail. "Can we get one someday?"

"I guess so," Harry sheepishly replied. The woman who owned the dog smiled at Harry.

"I love the dog's haircut. His name is Top Hat or Topsy for short." Brenda leaned down and the dog started licking her cheek. Brenda could charm anyone.

"They are wonderful dogs," the woman told Harry. "Not hard to care for at all. If you get a Scottish terrier you'll love it. You know, my husband was in the Royal Air Force. Unfortunately, he passed away two years ago. Your wife told me you were in the air force."

"I bet you miss your husband," Harry said.

"I do. Well, I better get going. Congratulations to you both." The woman walked towards the beach and the dog followed reluctantly. The dog kept turning and looking back for Brenda. It reminded Harry of how he would feel when Brenda went back to Connecticut.

"That dog loved you," Harry said.

"I love dogs. We used to have one when I was little. Those Scottish terriers are so cute. Come on, let's go to the store." Brenda grabbed Harry's arm and they began to walk again. Once they got to the store, he and Brenda purchased a leg of lamb, spices, and some potatoes. They also got a small chocolate cake for dessert. Harry loved the thought of having a home-cooked meal with Brenda. He often tired of the mess hall food. Brenda was a fantastic cook. He was a lucky man.

Back at the cottage, Harry went outside and lay down in a hammock in the garden with a magazine. He was so relaxed that he dozed on and off as he read. Then he fell asleep.

Harry awoke when he felt a kiss on his forehead.

"Come on, sleepyhead. Dinner's ready." The aroma of the lamb overpowered the house. The table was set and two long white candles were burning in the middle of the table. The food was set out on the table in serving dishes. There were plates, napkins, and silverware. Harry noticed that Brenda had on one of Mrs. McGregor's aprons. He teared up with happiness. He had wanted his own family for so long. He'd often been lonely since he's joined up. He was so happy to have Brenda in his life.

Chapter 77

"Can you believe we're both married?" Brenda said as she pushed Sophie in the stroller.

"I sure can't. I can't believe you got married in England on the spur of the moment. You are daring, but I am sure happy for you, Brenda. You're glowing. Harry's a lucky guy," Sarah said.

"Oh, Sarah. The honeymoon was awesome. I never thought I'd like sex as much as I did," Brenda said. Brenda had loved it and she missed Harry terribly. She couldn't wait to get back to him, but she was also torn at leaving her family and friends.

"Brenda, come on, no dirty talk," Sarah said. "You're pushing a baby."

"She doesn't know what I'm saying," Brenda said. She laughed. "Even if she did, look at sweet Sophie. She's smiling at me."

"I guess you're right," Sarah said.

"Right about what? Sophie not understanding us or sex being even better than expected?"

"Both," Sarah said as she burst into laughter. It made Brenda feel good to see Sarah laugh.

"Don't be a prude, sis. Don't you like sex?" Brenda asked.

"Of course I like it. I just don't like talking about it. I'm not as wild as you are," Sarah said. "I am going to miss you terribly though. Who's going to cheer me up when I'm down? I can't believe you're going all the way to England."

Brenda knew Sarah was having a hard time. Brenda was going to miss Sarah a lot too but Brenda had always wanted to travel the world. Now she could with Harry.

"I'll be back often and hopefully Harry will get transferred back to the states within a couple of years," Brenda said.

"A couple of years? Oh God. That seems like forever."

"Time will fly by, little sis. Plus, we can write and talk on the phone."

"I know. I'll just miss you," Sarah said. Brenda grabbed Sarah's hand and squeezed it.

"I'll miss you too. But you'll be busy. As well as Robert and Sophie, you'll have to look after Mom and Dad and Dylan too. Make sure Dylan doesn't sign up for the navy while I'm gone."

"I don't think he will. He'll at least finish school first. Plus, he adores Heather. She's good for him."

"I know. I love her," Brenda said. "Hey, let's keep walking all the way down to the Dairy Bar. I've craving ice cream."

Chapter 78

renda felt torn. She was due to leave for England in a week. She'd been home for three weeks and she totally missed Harry. Yet she was realizing how much she was going to miss her family. Hopefully Harry would get transferred back to the United States soon.

"Which one of your cousins is having this baby shower? I'm totally confused. And you said Harry already sent a gift?" Brenda asked. Eva Marie was driving her to Milltown to a baby shower at one of her relative's restaurants.

"Her name is Erica. She's a distant relative. Don't worry. I'll introduce you to everyone. There's the restaurant now." Eva Marie parked the car. The parking lot was full. The restaurant was brick and had white Christmas lights hanging across the front. She and Brenda got out and walked into the restaurant. Eva Marie didn't stop at the front hostess stand. She kept moving toward the back of the restaurant. Finally, Eva Marie turned and walked into a room that said private parties. Brenda followed. She looked around the room and everyone yelled, "Surprise."

Brenda burst into tears of happiness as she realized it was not only Harry's family that was present but her family and friends too. There was a table to her right that had photos of her wedding in England and photos of the ceremony at the register's office. There were pictures of her and Harry when they were little. Also on the table was a gorgeous rectangular cake with two layers, one smaller than the other. It was decorated with red roses, and in red writing it said, *Congratulations Harry and Brenda.* The colors matched the colors that they had had in England.

Sarah and Dylan came up to Brenda and hugged her. Sarah handed her a tissue to wipe her eyes. "What do you think, sis? Did we surprise you or what?"

"You guys are too much. I didn't suspect a thing." Brenda wiped her eyes. Robert came up holding baby Sophie and hugged Brenda. Brenda took baby Sophie into her arms. "I'm going to miss this little one."

Brenda noticed that Eva Marie was over giving Walter a kiss. What a fibber, Brenda thought. Eva Marie had told her that Walter was working tonight. Elizabeth, Eugene, and Harry's parents came up and surrounded her. Elizabeth said, "Congratulations, Brenda, you didn't think we'd let you move to England without throwing a party. Here, give me baby Sophie so you can greet your guests and meet Harry's family."

"Come on with me, sweetheart. I want to introduce you to all of our family." Harry's mom took Brenda's arm and guided her through the crowd, introducing her to people. Brenda got lots of kisses and people took photos. She wished Harry could be there to enjoy it. Everyone made her feel so welcome. Harry's mom dinged on a glass. Sarah handed Brenda a glass of champagne.

"Everyone. May I have your attention. Welcome as we celebrate Brenda and Harry's marriage. We wish Harry could be here, but he is off serving our country. Brenda leaves for England next week. We wish her a safe journey and we hope that she and Harry have a wonderful life together. We also hope for many grandchildren." Harry's mother winked at Brenda who laughed. The crowd toasted Brenda.

"Alright, everyone. There is a buffet set up on the side

wall over there. Please go help yourself," Harry's dad shouted and then he kissed Brenda on the top of the head. "You come with us to the family table."

Harry's dad led Brenda to a table at the front of the room. She was overwhelmed with how many people had come. Joe and Abbey came up to her as she passed by and wished her well. She thanked them for making the gorgeous cake. Henry, Laura, Heather, and Hazel were all there too. Even Robert's parents were there. She had heard they were still living in an apartment while their home was being rebuilt.

"Congratulations, Brenda," Hazel said. "Your sister is going to be beside herself without you around."

"I need you all to take care of her and baby Sophie while I'm gone. I'm going to miss all of you terribly."

"You know we'll miss you. You'll have such a neat adventure, Brenda. We're happy for you and Harry. Send us photos as you travel," Laura said.

Brenda caught up to Harry's dad. The family table was decorated beautifully. It seated Harry's parents, Brenda's parents, Brenda, Dylan, Robert, Sarah, and Heather. She smiled when she saw everyone together. The wait staff brought them dishes of food so they could eat family style. Brenda smiled as she thought of how wonderful her life with Harry would be.

Chapter 79

Elizabeth couldn't believe she was in New York staring at the SS United States. It would take Brenda five days to get to England. Brenda had her own room. Elizabeth felt relieved that Brenda had listened to her and wasn't flying.

The whole family had come down and stayed a night in New York so they could see Brenda off. Yesterday they had all gone to see the Statue of Liberty and then a matinee show of *Hello Dolly*. Then they had dinner at the restaurant on top of the hotel that Sarah and Robert had stayed in on their honeymoon. Elizabeth was proud of her family. They were not without their problems, but she loved them all and they were happy.

The porters had already taken Brenda's bags onto the boat. Brenda held baby Sophie in her arms. "You have to send me photos every month. I hate that I'll miss seeing her grow in person."

"Of course we'll send photos, Brenda. We sure are going to miss you," Robert said.

"Yeah, you know, Brenda, everyone's glad you're leaving on a ship rather than me," Dylan said.

"That sure is the truth." Sarah hugged Dylan. "You and your crazy navy idea. I'm relieved you're staying put."

"We're all glad you didn't enlist," Elizabeth said.

"I know, but I would like to serve my country someday.

However, one of us leaving the United States this year is enough."

"I'm going to miss you, Brenda." Eugene bent in and gave his daughter a hug. Tears streamed down his face.

"I'll miss you too, Dad." Brenda's heart felt like it was breaking.

"Bye, sis. Write as much as you can. I'm going to miss you," Sarah said.

"I'll miss you so much. Call me anytime. I'm here for you. Be strong. I'll write a lot and make sure to send me lots of photos and letters," Brenda whispered as mascara ran down her face.

"Brenda, be safe. Remember to call me when you get settled on the base. I'm going to worry until you get there. Harry is a lucky man to have you. I'll miss you." Elizabeth tried not to cry but Brenda noticed a few tears coming down her mom's face as she kissed her on the cheek. Just then the whistle blew, which meant that Brenda had to get on board. Families were scattered all around them saying their goodbyes.

"Bye, everyone." Brenda dried her tears with a tissue and kissed Sophie on the top of her head. "I better be going."

Brenda turned and walked toward the ship. Elizabeth's heart sank. Brenda turned and waved to them. Elizabeth felt a pain in her heart, but she wasn't afraid. It was just the pain a mother felt when a daughter leaves home.

Acknowledgements

Thanks to Uncle Bubby and Grandma Jessie for instilling in me the love of reading books at a young age. Much appreciation to Richard Krawiec for his inspiring fiction writing courses at the University of North Carolina-Chapel Hill. Much love to Michael, Maggie, my mom and dad, and all of my family and friends for their support and encouragement. A special thanks to Alison Williams for her excellent suggestions on how to make the book better and to Becky Eatmon for doing a thorough edit of the novel.